The Billionaire Next Door

The Sherbrookes of Newport

Christina Tetreault

DIGITAL ISBN: 978-0-9971118-9-7
PRINT ISBN:978-1548586980
:

OTHER BOOKS BY CHRISTINA

Dear Reader,

Thank you for once again visiting with the Sherbrooke family. When I started this book, I decided to bring everyone a little closer to my current home in New Hampshire and set much of the book here. All the New Hampshire towns mentioned in this book are towns located in and around me. Several of the places mentioned in the book, such as Polly's Pancake Parlor (which by the way does have the best pancakes anywhere), the Flume Gorge, and the Polar Caves are places I visit often with my family. Other business and attractions are based on actual places near me, but I have changed their names and in one instance its location.

I hope you enjoy your visit with the Sherbrookes.
Happy Reading
Christina

CHAPTER ONE

Curt Sherbrooke watched the real estate agent pull into the driveway behind his SUV. He'd worked with Peter Marcus in the past, and the man usually did a great job of finding just what he was looking for. He didn't expect this time to be any different.

"Nice to see you again," Peter said when he reached Curt. "I hope you didn't have too much trouble finding this place."

The rotaries in the center of town had confused his GPS. As a result, he'd gotten an unplanned tour of Pelham, New Hampshire. So far, he liked what he saw. The town appeared large enough for him to blend in and hopefully not draw too much attention to himself. At the same time, it wasn't so big it lost the essence of the traditional New England small town. It would be the perfect place to relax and work on his novel, while doing something he enjoyed.

"I got a little redirected along the way, but I managed. What did you find for me, Peter?" He checked out the house and grounds around him.

Peter opened the folder he held and pulled out a packet of papers. "This tells you all about the house and the town." He handed the packet to Curt. "I'll give you the basics for now. Originally, the house and the surrounding hundred acres belonged to the Draper family. They owned the quarry across the state line, in Dracut. The home stayed in the Draper family until the late 1940s. It's been sold twice since then. Thirty years ago, the current owners started selling off parcels of land, and many of houses you passed on the street were built. The last part of the original estate, the old groundskeeper's cottage, was sold twenty-five years ago. It's set way back, so you can't see it from the road. You would've passed its driveway on your way here. Today, the house comes with eight acres. The original stables remain on the property. The carriage house was converted into a three-car garage at some point, and there's a full apartment located above. The home has a heated in-ground pool and there's also a man-made pond on the property."

They walked up the cobblestone walkway. It, much like the exterior of the house, had seen better days. But Curt had expected as much. He had told Peter he was again in the market for a fixer-upper. If the exterior of the home was any indication, that was exactly what Peter had found him.

"According to the listing agent, the house needs a new heating system. What's in there right now works, but it's not efficient. You'd want to have something new installed before the winter. And there is no central air. A new roof was put on four years ago. Other than that, not much has been done here in a long time. The house has been empty for over two years." Peter retrieved the key from the lock box on the front door. "The listing agent is a friend of the owners. She told me the couple moved into an assisted living facility. None of their children want the old house, and at this point the couple needs the money from the sale to cover their expenses at the facility."

The hinges on the front door groaned when Peter opened it, and Curt stepped inside. The large wood-paneled foyer reminded him a bit of his grandparents' home. A faded mural covered the vaulted ceiling, and an antique chandelier with several bulbs out provided less than adequate light. An ornate stained-glass window filled the space above the front door, allowing in sunlight. Matching stained-glass panels flanked the door. A curving master staircase led up to the second floor, and two hallways stretched out to other parts of the home.

"The first floor contains the typical rooms you'd expect. There's also a ballroom located at the back of the house. Evidently, the Drapers liked to entertain when they lived here. Upstairs you'll find six bedrooms, as well as his and hers private offices and a billiard room. There's an elevator that goes between the first and second floors, however, it doesn't work. The listing agent isn't sure what is wrong with it."

"Let's look around," Curt said. From here he liked what he saw, but before he made a decision, he needed to see the rest of the house.

He went from room to room on the first floor, each one appearing to need more work than the one before it. Thankfully, it appeared much of it was cosmetic. There were no gaping holes in the ceilings or floors. All the windows looked old, but capable of keeping out the elements as well as any unwanted critters looking for a place to live. Even the kitchen appeared useable, if outdated. Nothing appeared to be a deal breaker.

Curt and Peter stopped in the ballroom last before heading upstairs. Much like in the foyer, a faded mural covered the ceiling. Old gilded mirrors hung around the room, and the wall above the fireplace was discolored, as if something had hung there for a long time before being taken down. Several well-worn area rugs covered the floor, making it difficult to gauge the condition of the floor underneath. Two full-size beds and two chests of drawers remained in the room, and Curt assumed the elderly couple had been using this as their bedroom rather than go up and down the stairs. Several sets of french doors still in remarkably good condition filled the exterior wall. Through the glass, Curt saw the large veranda. A patio table and chairs remained there, the table umbrella pitched at an odd angle and turned inside out. Everything he'd seen up until now suggested neither the family nor the listing agent had done much to improve the possibility the place would be sold. Honestly, it didn't matter much to him. He didn't want another magazine-worthy home. He already had several of those. No, he wanted a quiet place he could work on. A place he could bring back to life.

He'd gotten the bug to renovate homes five years ago. Laid up after a skiing accident, he'd gotten addicted to the home renovation shows on television. When he got back on his feet, he took several classes on carpentry and basic plumbing. He'd tackled his first project about three years ago, a small cottage in upstate New York. He'd picked it because the place hadn't needed much work, and he'd finished it in three months. Since then he'd purchased and worked on two other projects. Each had required more and more work. While there were still things he had to hire others to do, such as electrical work, he believed his own skills had vastly improved since the cottage in New York. He'd completed his most recent endeavor, a place in Marlborough, back in the fall, and was ready for a new challenge.

"Ready to head upstairs?" Peter asked, already back in the hallway.

Curt took one last look around the ballroom before nodding. At one time, the room must have been gorgeous. With some effort, it could be again. "Right behind you."

Much like the rooms below, occasional pieces of furniture lingered in the upstairs rooms, giving Curt the impression that family members had picked though what they wanted and left the rest behind for someone else to deal with. Dust and cobwebs filled each room, and again Curt wondered how the listing agent hoped to find a buyer given the condition of the house. Most people would take one look and walk right back out.

Structurally, the home appeared sound upstairs, too. A dark spot on a bedroom ceiling hinted at a leak, but it seemed contained to the one room. Since Peter had mentioned a new roof had been put on recently, Curt guessed the spot might have formed prior to then. Other than installing all new windows, and updating the electrical, Curt didn't see anything he either couldn't or wouldn't at least try handling himself anywhere in the house.

"There are a few rooms in the attic. I'm told the maids and the cook originally used them when the house belonged to the Draper family. Do you want to take a look?" Peter asked. They'd completed their tour of the entire second floor and stood near the staircase to the topmost level.

"No need. I've seen enough." Regardless of what he saw up on the third floor, he wouldn't change his mind. "I'm ready to make an offer. What's the asking price again?" Peter had given him the information over the phone, but he hadn't paid much attention to that particular detail.

Peter opened the folder he held before rattling off a figure.

"Sounds good. Let's go back to your office and do up the paperwork."

"You don't want to offer less? This house has a lot of potential, but it also needs a lot of work."

Curt had no idea what it cost for assisted living, but if what Peter told him was correct, the couple needed the money. Besides, it wasn't like he didn't have it. "I see no reason to waste time negotiating a figure. I'll offer the full asking price. Hopefully, we can get the sale done quickly. I'm eager to get started."

***

Rather than go straight back to Boston after leaving

Peter's office, he headed to his aunt and uncle's house so he could wish Aunt Marilyn a happy birthday. The call from his real estate agent confirming the owners had accepted his offer came as he turned in to Aunt Marilyn's driveway. According to Peter, the owners were just as eager to get the sale finalized, and the closing should happen within the month.

Curt parked next to two other cars. One had New York plates; he guessed his cousin Scott had driven up for a visit. The other had Rhode Island plates, so it could belong to any number of his relatives.

When he rang the doorbell, Scott answered, confirming Curt's original assumption. He held his nine-month-old son, Cooper, in his arms, and Curt noticed right away how much the baby had grown since he'd last seen him at Christmastime.

"Paige and Courtney are in the living room with my mom. I'll be back. Cooper needs a change," Scott said, referring to his girlfriend and younger sister.

"Better you than me," Curt said, slapping his cousin on the shoulder.

"Just wait. Your day will come, my friend." Scott carried his son upstairs, leaving Curt alone.

Curt didn't doubt it. When it came to marriage and having children, his cousins had been succumbing at an alarming rate. It'd started with his cousin Callie about three years ago and had continued steadily ever since. The most recent to tie the knot had been his cousin Derek. His cousin Gray's wedding was right around the corner. Curt guessed Scott and Paige would soon follow. While Scott hadn't asked Paige to marry him yet, she'd moved in with him the month before.

When Curt entered the room, the conversation paused, and all eyes focused on him. "Happy birthday, Aunt Marilyn," he said before greeting anyone else. He made his way through the minefield of baby toys on the floor so he could give her a hug.

Aunt Marilyn kissed his cheek and returned the embrace. "I'm so glad you stopped by. Scott's upstairs with Cooper. He'll be back in a minute."

"Yeah, I saw him. He let me in."

"Can you stay for dinner?" Aunt Marilyn asked. "Harrison isn't home yet, and he'll be disappointed if he misses you."

He had no place to be, and he wouldn't mind seeing his uncle today. He hadn't seen the man in several months. "Definitely."

Aunt Marilyn patted his knee and smiled. "Excellent. Judith said you've been house hunting again. Any luck?"

He'd never told Mom he was looking for a new project. It just hadn't come up during their last conversation. But he'd mentioned it to Dad. It'd been during the same conversation that he'd told the man he'd decided to leave his position at Nichols Investment in Boston. News his dad hadn't taken well.

"I made an offer on a place today. The closing should be soon."

"Where's this one?" Courtney, Curt's younger cousin, asked.

"New Hampshire... not far from the Massachusetts line."

"Why would you move all the way up there? Driving in and out of Boston when you want to work on it will be a pain the butt," Courtney said. "Couldn't you find anything closer?"

"I don't need to be in the city anymore. Friday was my last day at Nichols, so I'm going to live in this house while I do the renovations."

Scott walked in as Curt spoke. "You left the firm?" He set his son down amongst the toys. Cooper immediately crawled over to a stuffed dolphin and grabbed it. "I thought Burke was grooming you to take over his spot someday. Where are you working now?"

Jim Burke, the current CEO of Nichols Investment,

had been disappointed when Curt delivered the news. He'd offered him countless incentives to get him to stay. None had swayed him, though. He'd made up his mind. He, as well as the ulcer in his stomach, had had enough of the financial world and all the stress that went with it.

"Nowhere. At least for the foreseeable future, I'm going to work on the house I'm buying and finish my next novel."

"Next novel?" Courtney asked, pulling her attention away from her nephew. She'd moved from the couch to the floor to be with Cooper, and once he'd gotten the toy he'd wanted, he'd crawled into his aunt's lap.

Curt cringed.

"You still haven't told everyone?" Scott asked, noticing his expression.

"Tell everyone what?" Courtney demanded.

She was the only one in the room who didn't know that truth. When his first book came out and hit all the major lists, he'd shared the news with Scott as well as a few other members of the family. He'd written the novel under a pen name, and he worried that if too many people knew, his true identity would come out.

He'd have to add one more name to the list of people who knew about his alter ego. "About a year ago, a book I wrote came out. It did well and my agent got me a deal for another four. I'm almost finished with the second."

"How did I miss this?" Courtney asked.

"I used a pen name. When I submitted the manuscript, not even the agent knew my real name." When his agent had learned the truth, she'd been speechless.

Courtney blinked several times, and he suspected he knew the question headed his way. "Why did you do that?"

"Why do you think, genius?" Calling his cousin a genius wasn't far from the truth. Courtney Belmont was perhaps the most intelligent person he knew. She had an IQ of 154 and had completed high school two years early, then gone on to graduate from both Harvard and Yale in record time. Despite all her intelligence, sometimes she missed the most obvious… like now.

"I wanted the book published because it was good, not because of who I am. And I definitely didn't want people buying it because the name Sherbrooke was on the front cover."

Courtney rolled her eyes at him. "I assumed as much. But it'll get out. You know it will. Someone who knows, either at the publishing house or maybe even your agent, will let it slip. Why bother wasting the time to keep it a secret, especially now if the book is out and people like it?"

He recognized that what Courtney said was very possible. Still, he preferred to keep the truth under wraps for as long as he could.

"People didn't just like it, Courtney. Curt's book hit *all* the major lists. Our dear cousin is a fantastic writer. I'm looking forward to his next one," Scott said, joining the conversation.

"You and my publisher. She expects the manuscript no later than August tenth."

On the floor, Courtney accepted the stuffed dolphin Cooper handed her. "Guess I'd better get your first book. What name did you use?"

"C.S. Hilton." He'd struggled with a good pen name. Finally, he'd opted to go with his initials and his mother's maiden name.

"That's you?" Courtney sounded amazed. "I couldn't put *Fatal Deception* down. I finished it in two nights."

"Neither could I," Aunt Marilyn chimed in. She'd already known about his secret career. His mom had told her not long after the book was released. "And I can't wait for the next one. Even your uncle enjoyed it, and you know he never reads fiction."

"You shouldn't have to wait too much longer. For the next few months all I plan on doing is writing and working on the new house." And the town of Pelham, New Hampshire, would be the perfect place. He'd be away from all major distractions. And if people did eventually realize who he was, hopefully it wouldn't be until he finished the renovations and was ready to move on.

***

Exhausted, Taylor Walker popped open the trunk and pulled out the bag containing her body armor. She'd left the house before the sun came up. Coffee and sugar had kept her going much of the day, but she'd passed the point where either would do any more good. As a DEA agent in Boston, working crazy hours wasn't anything new or unusual. Unfortunately, it would take her body a couple days to feel normal again. Every once in a while, she wondered why she'd left the Boston Police Department and gone to work for the Drug Enforcement Agency instead. Then she'd be part of a successful bust like today, and she'd remember. Yes, drugs and drug dealers were still out there, but thanks to the work she and her colleagues did this morning there were fewer tonight.

"Auntie Taylor." Reese, Taylor's niece, skipped down the driveway, her ponytail swaying from side to side. "I made something for you at school today."

Taylor put her gear down and gave Reese a hug.

"Most kids made it for their moms. Hazel is saving hers and giving it to her nana for her birthday. But I wanted it to be for you."

"I can't wait to see it."

Once again, she wished she could catch the jerk who'd first introduced her older sister, Reese's mother, to drugs. Reese should be making things for her mom, like her friends at school. But she wasn't. Instead, she was living with her aunt and grandmother while her mom was who knew where, doing God knew what.

"We're having tacos for dinner. Mimi let me cut up the tomatoes." Reese loved tacos. The kid would eat them or pizza every day if they let her.

Taylor picked up her body armor and the duffel bag containing the clothes she'd worn to work that morning.

After a big arrest and search like today, she always showered and changed her clothes back at the office before she came home.

"Can I carry something?"

Taylor passed the duffel bag to her niece. While Reese was strong for an almost- seven-year-old, the body armor still weighed fifty pounds, not to mention the bag was cumbersome. "So how was school today? Did you do anything fun?"

"Great. The butterflies in class hatched this morning. It was kind of gross. Mrs. Lowell says it'll be a few days before we release them outside. I wish we didn't have to. I like having them in class."

Taylor didn't remember ever having caterpillars change into butterflies in her first-grade classroom. Then again, a lot of the things Reese did in class were different from when she'd been in school.

"They won't survive if you don't release them."

"Mrs. Lowell told us that. I still wish they could stay. Butterflies are pretty." Reese opened the front screen door and stepped inside. "Mimi, Auntie Taylor is home," she called, loud enough for their neighbors down the street to hear.

Priscilla Walker, Taylor's mother, poked her head around the corner. "I know, I saw her car in the driveway. Dinner's ready if you're hungry, Taylor."

Her mom knew it wasn't uncommon on days like today for her to not get a chance to eat all day. Often, that meant a stop at the first fast-food restaurant she saw on the way home because she was so hungry she could no longer wait. Thankfully, today had been a little different. She'd managed a light lunch after the arrest. "Starving, and I heard we're having tacos."

"Reese made sure to remind me today is Taco Tuesday. Everything is on the table. Have a seat. I'll be right in. Don't wait for me to get started." Priscilla disappeared again, and Taylor heard the bathroom door close.

When Priscilla joined them a few moments later, Reese already had her first taco assembled, although Taylor refused to let her niece start eating until Priscilla joined them.

Reese picked up her taco as soon as her grandmother sat down, but then she paused before taking a bite. "Mrs. Hewitt sent home something about career day tomorrow. She told me to give it to you. It's in my folder."

Taylor closed her eyes. She'd forgotten all about career day tomorrow morning. Every year since the new superintendent took office, they did a career day at each of the town schools. This year, Mrs. Hewitt, the elementary school principal, had asked her to participate, and she'd agreed. Too many kids believed working for the DEA or any other government agency was something only men could do. She hoped taking part in career day would show girls it was definitely an option for them when they graduated from school.

"I'll get it after dinner."

"You'll never guess what happened today," Priscilla said while Reese munched away and Taylor prepared her first two tacos. "Kimberly called me. She and David accepted an offer on the house."

"About time."

Kimberly and David Cranston had moved out of the huge house next door and into an assisted living facility a good two years ago. Since then the place had remained empty, slowly deteriorating from the beautiful house Taylor remembered it being when she was young to the run-down property she passed when she went running.

"I hope they got enough for it," Taylor said.

Although fifteen years separated Kimberly Cranston and Priscilla, the two women were good friends. When the Cranstons put the house on the market, she'd confided in Priscilla that without the money from the sale, they wouldn't be able to stay in their current location long. Considering how long ago they'd moved, Taylor assumed the Cranstons were getting close to being forced to move again. And Taylor knew the Cranstons' children would never help. Although all very successful, they were three of the most self-centered people she knew. They rarely even went to visit their parents, never mind help them financially.

"According to Kimberly, they got the full asking price," Priscilla answered.

"Who'd be willing to pay that much?" Taylor loved the old house next door. It was a one of a kind gem in town, but the house needed a lot of work both inside and out. Even before the Cranstons moved out, it had needed stuff done. The years of neglect since then hadn't helped any.

Priscilla gave a slight shrug. "Kimberly didn't know much about the gentleman, other than he's currently living in Boston. She told me he also agreed to skip a house inspection before the sale is finalized."

It pleased her to hear the place had been sold, but she feared the new owner might have a few screws loose. Skip a house inspection on that old place? Who in their right mind would do that, especially after looking at the house?

"Maybe someone with children will move in," Taylor said.

While her niece had plenty of friends, none lived on the street. When she and Eliza had been growing up, many of the houses near them contained children their age. Now, though, Reese was the only elementary-school-age child on the entire street. Instead, all their neighbors either had grown children who had moved out, or babies.

"I was thinking the same thing myself. The house is simply too big for a single person. Whoever bought it must either have children or be planning to start a family."

She agreed, but then whoever bought the house might not plan on keeping it. Other homes in and around town had been purchased, fixed up, and then immediately put on the market again. A small two-bedroom on Sawmill Road, in fact, had been sold the past fall, and after being gutted and spruced up it went back on the market in March. A sale pending sign had gone up in front of it last week.

"Did Mrs. Cranston say when the closing might be?" Taylor asked.

"No, we didn't talk long. She had other calls to make. But I'll see her next week and I'll ask." Priscilla and Mrs. Cranston attended a book club together every other Thursday night.

Across the table, Reese polished off her second taco and started building a third, a bottomless pit when it came to food. With a break in the adults' conversation, she decided to add her own news. "Stripes caught a mouse."

Stripes was the American Shorthair cat they'd found in the shed three winters ago. At the time, Taylor had feared the animal wouldn't make it through the week. He'd surprised them all, though, and while he spent much of his time inside, he did occasionally venture outside on warm, sunny days like today.

"He left it on the patio under the table," Reese added.

Well, at least he hadn't brought it inside. He'd tried to do that a time or two. Thankfully, she'd always caught him before he left it somewhere in the house.

"I'll take care of it after dinner." While death was a part of life, she didn't want her young niece seeing a mouse decompose.

"Deb came into the library this morning," Mom said, once her granddaughter went back to stuffing herself with tacos. "Her son, Jack, is moving back to town this month."

Already Taylor didn't like the sound of this particular conversation.

"I guess he hated living in Colorado. It was his wife who wanted to move there. His divorce is final now, and he found a new position with the Manchester police department."

Yep, she knew what her mother intended here.

"Deb and I thought you two should go for coffee or

something. You have a lot in common. And you're both single."

Her mom loved to play matchmaker. She'd gone on her fair share of dates, thanks to Mom's past efforts.

"I remember Jack from high school, Mom. I'm not interested in going for coffee or anything else with him." In high school, Jack had been a bully. There really was no other word to describe him. Maybe he'd changed over the last sixteen years, but she didn't care to find out.

"Just think about it. You haven't gone out with anyone in a while."

For some reason, Mom believed a woman needed a man by her side to be happy. Maybe it was because she'd had such a great marriage. But Taylor didn't agree. As far as she saw it, if the right man came along, great; if not, she was okay staying single.

"What about—"

Before Mom finished, Taylor interrupted her, something she tried to avoid, especially in front of her niece. However, she needed to catch this before Mom's enthusiasm really got going. "Mom, please don't set me up with anyone. We've talked about it before. I'm capable of finding my own dates. I don't need you to do it for me."

Mom pouted. "I just want you to be happy like your father and I were. That'll never happen if you don't date."

Taylor realized that and appreciated it. But it didn't change her mind on the subject. "I know, Mom. But, really, I can handle it."

"Hazel told me her dad has a new girlfriend," Reese said, jumping into the conversation and saving Taylor from Mom's further insistence.

Taylor glanced at Mom because, as far as she knew, Hazel's father was married to Hazel's mother. Or at least they had been back in September when school started. When Mom shrugged, Taylor guessed she didn't know anything either.

"Hazel's dad doesn't live with her anymore. He lives in

a different house, but she has a room there for when she visits."

She'd realized not long after Reese started talking that kids held nothing back. If they thought your shirt was ugly, or you looked like hell, they let you know. It sounded like it also applied to when your parents separated. Once again, Taylor was pleased they'd decided not to tell Reese the complete truth about her mom and why she wasn't around. Since Reese had not even been a year old when she was taken from Eliza, she had no memories of the woman. Someday they'd have to tell her everything. She had a right to know the truth. It wasn't a conversation Taylor was looking forward to having."

CHAPTER TWO

Curt stored the empty suitcases in the bedroom closet. He'd signed the purchase and sale agreement the previous week, and immediately hired a company to come in and remove all the items left behind in the house. With all the stuff gone, he needed to decide where he wanted to begin renovations. The house inspection conducted two days ago confirmed what he already suspected: the building was structurally sound, so he didn't have to worry about the house falling down around his head. He had appointments set up with two HVAC companies to come in and give him estimates for updating the entire heating system and installing central air conditioning. The estimates for updating the electrical should be in any day. And he planned to set up appointments with window companies in the near future. Aside from those three major items, he hoped to complete everything himself. It would take a while, but time was something he had plenty of these days.

Switching off the bedroom light, he closed the door behind him. He'd spent the last few hours settling into one of the bedrooms. Although one of the smaller rooms, he'd chosen it because it needed the least amount of work for now. Once he finished the master bedroom down the hall, he'd relocate into it. He'd also set up his office today so he could get back to work on the book. It hadn't been difficult deciding which office to use. Although the more masculine of the two rooms was larger, it also reeked of smoke. Curt assumed the former owner had done all his smoking in there and outside, because he couldn't detect the smell anywhere else. Even if the room hadn't smelled so bad, he may have picked the more feminine office. Located in the back of the house, the room was farther from the street and overlooked the backyard.

Since he was somewhat settled, now seemed as good a time as any to decide where he wanted to start with the renovations.

Downstairs, he pushed open a door on his left and flipped up the wall switch. The overhead bulb went on for a moment or two before it went dead. Curt made a mental note to change all the light bulbs as soon as possible, even in those light fixtures he planned to replace at some point. The window near the toilet in the first-floor bathroom allowed in enough natural light. Although extremely outdated, it was functional and definitely not a number-one priority on his list, much like the library and upstairs in the home's billiard room. Both those rooms only needed fresh coats of paint and new light fixtures.

Curt closed the bathroom door and went down to the kitchen. This seemed like the most logical place to start. While he didn't love to cook, he did when necessary. If he planned on living in the house indefinitely, he'd need to prepare food. With the warmer months here, he could throw a grill outside and do most of his cooking there until he finished renovating the kitchen. On the days he couldn't grill, take-out was an option. He already had a decent idea of what he wanted to do in here, too.

Although somewhat smaller in size, the room was laid out much like his cousin's kitchen in Newport before

Trent had it remodeled. Trent's wife, an interior designer, had turned the kitchen there from a place designed for servants to prepare food into a gourmet kitchen the entire family could gather in. While Curt didn't intend to live here long enough for his family to gather, whomever he sold the house to would.

The light bulb over the kitchen sink went out. Never mind changing the bulbs as soon as possible, he'd change them tonight before he found himself walking around in the dark. During his drive into town, he'd passed a hardware store on Route 38, just down the street from the grocery store. He could head over that way now and kill both errands, because while he'd eaten breakfast before leaving Boston, he'd need to eat again today. When he got back, he'd arrange for a dumpster to be delivered so he could start tearing apart this room, something he was looking forward to. Honestly, he enjoyed the demolition aspect of renovation almost as much as the rebuilding process. Swinging a sledgehammer against something solid gave him a sense of satisfaction he'd never experienced while wearing a suit and sitting in an office.

Assuming he'd go out today at some point, he'd left his SUV parked in front of the house rather than in the garage. He'd been pleased when the building inspector assured him the converted carriage house was safe to use. Even so, he'd left his favorite cars in the garage at his Newport condo and had only his motorcycle delivered here.

A black, white, and gray cat sat on the vehicle's hood when he walked outside. The cat followed Curt with his eyes as he walked around the front of the SUV. When Curt stopped and held out his hand, the cat twitched its tail. "Hey there."

The cat meowed and remained still as Curt ran a hand down his back. "Where do you belong, my friend?" Again the cat twitched its tail, but made no indication he planned to move from his chosen spot in the sun.

Careful not to spook the animal, Curt slowly picked it up. The cat looked well cared for, and had a bright orange collar around its neck. He reached for the heart-shaped ID tag attached to the collar. "Stripes," he said. "The name fits you." Curt flipped the tag over. An address and phone number were printed on the back. "You belong next door."

Should he bring the cat home? Some people allowed their cats to roam freely, confident they'd come home when ready. Others never allowed them outside. Curt had no idea which Stripes here was. He'd feel awful if it turned out Stripes wasn't an outdoor cat, but had instead slipped out. And he would have to meet his neighbors eventually. Even if he didn't have much interaction with them, at some point they'd cross paths. "Looks like you're getting a ride home, Stripes."

Stripes didn't hesitate to curl up in the passenger seat when Curt set him down.

A long, winding driveway brought Curt down to a small house. The exterior of it reminded him of the house he'd bought, which made sense. Peter had mentioned this home had once been the groundskeeper's cottage when the Drapers owned the property. Although the home was as old as his, this one had been maintained over the years. Even the lawn and plants in front looked well cared for.

Curt parked behind a white Chevy Malibu. A girl's bike rested against the front steps, but the door was closed. "I hope someone is home." He gave the cat a scratch behind the ear before ringing the doorbell.

It didn't take long for someone to answer. A woman perhaps in her late fifties or early sixties opened the door. Before either of them could speak, a young girl's voice called out, "Is it the mailman, Mimi?" A moment later, the owner of the voice skidded to a stop at the door.

"What are you doing with Stripes?" the girl demanded when she saw him there.

"Reese Walker, that's no way to greet someone," the

older woman, who he assumed was a relative judging by the resemblance, said before she turned her attention to him again.

He offered up a smile. "Don't worry about it. It's a fair question," Curt said, before holding the cat toward the little girl. "I found him sitting on my car next door. I wasn't sure if he'd gotten out by mistake."

"Stripes likes to walk around outside, but he usually stays in our yard," the older woman said, giving the cat a pat on the head. "You must be the one who bought the Cranston house. Welcome to town. I'm Priscilla, and this is my granddaughter, Reese." She extended her hand toward him.

"Curt, and that'd be me. I moved in today." He shook her hand and waited for any sign she recognized him. Although he resembled his mother's side of the family more than his father's, he still had the Sherbrooke blue eyes like his dad and so many of his cousins. And he'd had his fair share of pictures in magazines. Thankfully, nothing like his cousins Jake and Trent, though. In an effort to help conceal his identity, he'd stopped shaving, so a well-trimmed beard now covered his face. He'd skipped his last two scheduled haircuts as well. As an extra measure, he'd thrown on a pair of eyeglasses.

"I thought I saw the moving trucks go by. You're probably not done unpacking yet. Why don't you join us for dinner tonight? We're making lasagna. There's more than enough for an extra few guests."

"It's just me next door." He hadn't anticipated dinner invitations from his neighbors. The woman appeared friendly, and he hated to be rude. "Sure, sounds great. Thank you. Can I bring anything?"

Priscilla shook her head. "No, just yourself. We usually eat around seven."

"I'll see you then."

***

Taylor locked her gun in the bedroom safe before

going back downstairs. While she'd drilled gun safety into her niece, she saw no point in taking any chances. She noticed the extra plate on the table as soon as she entered the kitchen.

"Who's coming for dinner?" They never had last-minute guests, and she didn't remember Mom mentioning company tonight.

"Our new neighbor. He found Stripes this afternoon and brought him home. Moving and unpacking is draining. I thought he'd like a meal he didn't have to prepare himself, so I invited him to join us."

Taylor looked toward the ceiling and shook her head. "You invited a stranger to eat with us?" Sometimes her mom's heart was just too damn big.

Mom left the salad she was preparing and went to the refrigerator. "Curt's not a stranger. He lives next door. Besides, he looked harmless."

How many times had she heard something similar from victims? More than enough to know looks could be deceiving.

"Peppers or mushrooms in the salad tonight?" Mom asked, her back still turned to Taylor.

"Either is fine." The contents of their salad didn't concern her. Having a strange man eat dinner with her niece did. "I really wish you'd waited to invite him, given everyone a chance to get to know him."

"Why? So you could run a background check on him first?" Her mom chuckled and took out the peppers and mushrooms.

Mom might laugh, but if she could run a background check on the man, she would. Unfortunately, doing so without a valid reason was an agency no-no.

"Would an ax murderer return a cat to his home? Relax, Taylor. He won't kill us over dinner."

Her mom would be surprised the things criminals did to make their victims feel at ease and invite them into their homes. Belaboring the point wouldn't change the fact their neighbor was joining them. Taylor considered whether or not to go back upstairs and get her gun. Dressed in denim capris and a tank top, there would be no way to conceal it unless she pulled on a baggy sweatshirt. It was a gorgeous spring evening, and Mom had all the windows open. Both their guest and niece would find it odd if she sat down with a big sweatshirt on. Their guest might not question it, but Reese wouldn't think twice about saying something.

"What time is he coming?"

"He should be here any minute. I told him we eat around seven," Mom answered, just as the doorbell rang and the oven timer went off. "Perfect timing. Can you get the lasagna, and I'll get the door?" She didn't stick around for an answer. She wiped her hands on a dishtowel and walked out of the kitchen.

"Thank you, but really, you didn't have to bring anything." Her mom's voice traveled the short distance from the front door into the kitchen. "Come on in. Dinner is ready."

"It smells delicious, Mrs...." A deep male voice, perhaps the sexiest she'd ever heard, reached Taylor from the hallway.

"Walker, but please call me Priscilla. We're neighbors. There's no need to be so formal."

Mom and their new neighbor entered the kitchen, and Taylor did a quick assessment of the man. He appeared to be around her age, although the sexy, barely there beard could be making him appear older than he was. He had brown hair, the ends of which were almost brushing against the collar of his T-shirt. Even with the wire-rimmed glasses she could tell his eyes were an incredible shade of blue. His dark blue T-shirt stretched across broad shoulders, and the short sleeves revealed muscular arms. Even without X-ray vision she suspected the T-shirt covered a great body. Taylor didn't let her visual inspection go any further.

"Curt, this is my daughter, Taylor." Mom handed her

the bottle of wine she held. "Can you open this while I go tell Reese dinner's ready?" She didn't wait for an answer before she glanced back toward their guest. "Please have a seat. I'll be right back."

Not very smooth, Mom. Despite their conversation weeks ago, it looked like Mom was ready to play matchmaker again. "You got it," she answered, even though it wasn't necessary. "Would you like some lemonade or water?" No matter how she felt about having a dinner guest, there was no need to be rude to him.

"Water sounds good, thanks."

The sound of his voice could only be described in one way: sensual. It was the type of voice associated with a sexy late-night radio DJ. Listening to him talk over dinner wouldn't be a hardship at all. Neither would looking at him. Wow, the man was handsome.

Reese dominated the conversation as everyone else started dinner, by filling the adults in on the excitement that occurred at recess. First, a boy in her grade decided it would be more fun to jump from the top of the slide rather than go down it. He'd been taken off the playground in a wheelchair, his arm at a funny angle. Not long afterward, a snake was found sunning himself underneath a basketball hoop. Many of the girls and a few boys ran screaming from it. Of course Reese, being Reese, had gone in for a closer look and only left when the recess monitor ordered everyone away from it.

With the day's excitement shared, Reese worked on filling her stomach, leaving the adults a chance to talk for the first time since sitting down.

"Where did you live before coming here?" Mom asked.

Taylor knew Mom already knew the answer, but suspected she didn't want their guest to know she'd talked to Kimberly Cranston about him. Although, from what Mom told her, Kimberly hadn't shared much information about the man now seated at their table.

"I've lived in Boston for the past five years."

She'd suspected he wasn't originally from the Boston area. Normally people who'd spent their entire lives in the city had a distinct Bostonian accent. Working in the city, she heard it all the time. Curt's voice held no hint of it. Actually, she couldn't detect any accent at all when he spoke.

"Taylor used to live in Boston. Well, Watertown actually. Do you work in Boston?" Priscilla asked.

"I did, but I recently left the investment firm I worked for."

"Auntie Taylor works in Boston," Reese said, deciding she needed to join the conversation again. "She's a DEA agent. She took me to her office once to meet her friends."

Curt glanced her way, his surprise evident, then he looked back at Reese. "Your aunt does important work." He turned his incredible blue eyes on her again. Even with the glasses he was an extremely handsome man, but she suspected he'd be gorgeous without them. "Have you worked for the agency long?"

"Almost eight years." Wow, had it really been that long already? She quickly double-checked her math. She'd started her training down in Quantico a week before her twenty-sixth birthday, and in two weeks she'd be thirty-four. *Yep, almost eight years.*

"What brought you to Pelham? A new job?" Taylor asked. Conducting a background check was out, but she'd like to know as much as possible about the man now living next to them.

"I needed a change. Someplace quiet. I'm writing a book, and sometimes the city is too much of a distraction."

"Mimi works at the library. Do you have a book there?" Reese asked.

Curt frowned and cleared his throat. Obviously, he didn't like Reese's question, and Taylor wondered why.

"It's possible. But you'd find it boring."

"An author living right next door. What's the title?

Maybe I've read it," Mom said.

Unlike her, Mom was an avid reader. She devoured both fiction and nonfiction books. She'd tried to pass her love of reading on to both Taylor and her older sister, but neither had taken to it. Reading meant she had to sit down in one place. Instead, she'd been much more interested in math. In fact, both her parents encouraged her to study mathematics in college rather than criminal justice and psychology. Neither of her parents had wanted her to follow her in her father's footsteps. But she'd decided in middle school she wanted to be a police officer like Dad. Only later, when Eliza got arrested the first time for drugs, had she decided to apply to the DEA.

Again, Curt appeared uncomfortable before he answered, "*Fatal Deception.*"

She'd never heard of it, but judging by her mom's expression, she had. Her face reminded Taylor of a teen meeting their favorite pop star.

"You're C.S. Hilton? We couldn't keep copies of the book in the library. It was wonderful, by the way. Marion isn't going to believe me when I tell her C.S. Hilton is living in town. Maybe you can come and do a reading at the library one night."

"Actually, Priscilla, I'd really appreciate it if you didn't share the information with anyone. When people learned where I lived in Boston, I started getting strange things in the mail. Random people would stop by and wait for me to leave my building. I'd really like to avoid that if possible."

Mom nodded immediately. "We don't want that around here. Don't worry, we won't tell anyone. Right, Reese?"

Reese could keep a secret; you just needed to tell her upfront that whatever she'd heard couldn't be shared, otherwise she'd tell anyone anything.

Reese paused between bites and nodded. "I wish you wrote kids' books instead."

While Mom had failed to instill a love of reading in her

daughters, she'd succeeded with her granddaughter. Reese had learned to read before starting kindergarten and now devoured books written for children older than her. Thank goodness for a well-stocked town library, otherwise they'd be at the bookstore every other day buying more books.

"Have you started getting estimates for the work on the house?" Taylor asked. The man was obviously uncomfortable talking about his book. The house seemed like a safer, less intrusive topic. "If you haven't already, you should give Baker and Sons Construction a call. They're located here in town."

She'd gone to school with Ryan Baker, the older of the two sons. Although Mr. Baker was still involved, Ryan had taken over the business after his dad suffered a heart attack. Unlike his younger brother, who'd moved to California, Ryan was one of the hardest-working people she knew, and thorough. He expected the same from the people who worked for him. When you hired Baker and Sons for a job, it got done right.

"Thanks for the recommendation. I'm hoping to do most of the work myself. It's kind of a hobby of mine. But if I run into any problems, I'll give them a call."

"You'll want to check out 38 Lumber and Hardware. It's over near the grocery store. Dad refused to go anywhere else. And he was always working on something around here."

Across the table, Mom gave a little laugh. "My late husband was always taking something apart and putting it back together. Often, Taylor would be working right alongside him. Taylor and her dad built the bookcase in the living room together when she was seven. And she helped him remodel the upstairs bathroom when she was in middle school."

Curt glanced at Taylor again. The woman intrigued him. She was nothing like the women he came in contact with on a daily basis, and definitely nothing like the

27

women he was usually attracted to. Strength and confidence radiated from her. No doubt about it, Taylor Walker was a woman who could take care of herself no matter the situation. Although she worked in a male-dominated field, the butterfly earrings she wore, and the light pink nail polish on her fingernails suggested she had a softer feminine side. She'd tied up her chestnut-colored hair, so he had no way of telling its length, but he guessed when down her hair would fall below her shoulders. And at about five seven or eight, she had a killer body, which he'd noticed the moment he walked into the kitchen.

"If I get stuck on something, maybe I'll enlist Taylor's help," he said. Honestly, he could see himself asking Taylor for help on a lot of things, and none of them had anything to do with remodeling his house.

"I don't know, Mr. Author, you might not be able to afford me." Her voice carried a hint of laughter. It was the most relaxed she'd sounded all night.

A heavy dose of guilt smacked him in the gut. They'd accepted without question that he was nothing more than C.S. Hilton, the author of *Fatal Deception*. And it wasn't as if he had completely lied to them, but telling him he was also Curt Sherbrooke, the nephew of the president of the United States and a member of the wealthiest family in the country, wasn't an option. As it was, he wasn't certain they could keep what he had shared a secret. He hadn't seen any other choice when he'd told them he was an author. The fewer lies he told, the less likely he was to slip and make a mistake if they spoke in the future. Something told him he'd be seeing Taylor, Priscilla, and Reese Walker again.

"I guess I'd better find the number for Baker and Sons."

"Can I skate on your pond this winter?" Reese asked. She'd finished her food but stayed at the table, listening to the conversation.

"Mr. and Mrs. Cranston used to let the neighborhood

kids ice skate on the pond behind your house. Even after they moved, they let us bring Reese back there to skate," Taylor said, explaining her niece's request.

At least as long as he lived there, he saw no problem with it. Once he finished the house and moved on in a year or so, they could take it up with the new owners. "Sure... as long as you have an adult with you."

"I think you're going to love living here," Priscilla said. "It's a great place to raise a family. Both my daughters grew up here."

"Do you have any kids?" Reese asked, sounding hopeful. "All the kids on the street are babies. My best friend, Hazel, lives near school when she's with her mom. When she stays with her dad, she lives somewhere else. I don't know where. I'd like someone next door to play with."

"Sorry, no kids. I don't even have a pet."

"Do you have a girlfriend? Hazel's dad has a new girlfriend. She really likes her. She lets Hazel play with her makeup when she stays over. Hazel said her mom doesn't have a boyfriend, but she talks on the phone a lot to someone."

Did all children Reese's age ask questions like that? The only children he spent any time around still wore diapers. "Uh, no girlfriend either. I'm all alone next door."

Reese smiled, revealing the missing bottom tooth. "Maybe Auntie Taylor can be your girlfriend. I always hear Mimi telling her she should go out more."

He heard Taylor softly groan, and suddenly her face matched her fingernails. Curt wasn't sure if he should groan too, or laugh. Both reactions fit the current conversation. And as embarrassing as the conversation had suddenly turned, Reese's comments answered a question he'd had but couldn't ask himself. Taylor Walker was single.

"Reese, if you're done eating, why don't you go upstairs, get ready for bed, and then do some reading,"

Taylor said.

Curt guessed she was afraid her niece would either share some other embarrassing information or ask a question better not asked.

Reese ducked under the table. When she reappeared, she had Stripes in her arms. He hadn't even realized the cat was under the table. "*Yes*, I don't have to help clean the table tonight!" She hightailed it out of the kitchen without another word to anyone.

"Sorry about that," Taylor said once Reese was gone. "She'll be seven in June, and often doesn't think before she asks questions."

Curt shrugged. "Don't worry about it. She can ask me anything. Not much embarrasses me."

"Anyone interested in some dessert?" Priscilla asked, perhaps as a way to change the subject. "Reese and I made some oatmeal cookies after school today."

"All set, Mom."

"Thank you, but I couldn't eat another thing," Curt answered. "Dinner was delicious."

Priscilla pushed back her chair and stood up. "In that case, I'm going to make sure Reese did what she was supposed to before she starts reading." She left the kitchen almost as quickly as her granddaughter.

Curt and Taylor looked at each other, and he struggled not to smile. "She left us alone on purpose, didn't she?" Curt asked.

Taylor sighed. "Yeah, probably. But it's not unusual for us to tell Reese to get ready for bed, and instead she sits down and starts reading. The girl is a bookworm."

If his mother or one of his aunts did something similar, he'd be beyond annoyed. Tonight, it didn't faze him. "I can picture my mom doing the same thing."

He considered his next sentence before he opened his mouth. He'd moved here with a simple plan: keep to himself, work on his house, and finish his book. Right now he wanted to add a fourth item to his plan: get to know the sexy DEA agent living next door. If he kept it very casual, she never needed to know who he really was.

"Would you like to go for coffee sometime?" Taylor asked the question before he could.

"Name the day and time."

CHAPTER THREE

"Auntie Taylor, you look pretty."

Taylor looked over at Reese standing in the bedroom doorway. "Thanks. How'd the game go?" Reese had made the town's travel soccer team this year. She loved it, even though her best friend Hazel wasn't playing with her. Instead, Hazel had decided to play softball like her older sister, a sport Reese found boring.

"We won. I scored the only goal. I wish you'd been there." Reese came into the room, and made herself comfortable on the bed where Stripes was already curled up in a patch of sunlight.

Taylor tried to make it to as many of Reese's games as possible. She had planned on going to this one, too, but a last-minute development in one of her cases had kept her from getting home until three o'clock this morning. Getting up in time to get Reese to the soccer field in New Ipswich for her nine o'clock game had been out of the question, so Mom drove her.

"I should be there next week. Did you and Mimi stop to eat after the game?"

"Reese wanted to wait and see if you wanted to come with us," Mom said from the doorway.

Taylor leaned over and ruffled her niece's hair. "Thanks for thinking of me, but I have to pass this time. I'm having coffee with Curt in a little while."

Reese bounced up and down on the bed. "I like him. He's cute. Can I come with you?"

She'd expected a different response from Reese. Frequently, the three of them would stop for pizza or burgers after a soccer game. Sometimes they'd grab ice cream, too, before coming home.

"You can't leave me all alone. Besides, we'll have more fun than Aunt Taylor. Maybe we'll even stop for ice cream after lunch." Mom walked into the room.

"Can I get a waffle cone?" Reese asked, forgetting all about going with Taylor at the possibility of getting ice cream, one of her favorite treats.

Mom took her time before answering. "I think we can arrange that. But first go wash up and change your clothes." Reese still wore her soccer uniform, minus her cleats. "Don't forget to get your face, too. Not just your hands and arms."

No one had to tell her twice. Reese jumped off the bed, waking Stripes up in the process. After the cat verified nothing was wrong, though, he twitched his tail and again closed his eyes. "'Bye, Auntie Taylor. Love you."

With Reese gone, Taylor waited for Mom's questions. She didn't need to wait long.

"Having coffee with Curt? When did this come about?" Mom took the spot Reese had vacated on the bed, a clear indication she planned to ask several questions.

To avoid having Mom bring it up countless times over the past few days, Taylor had decided not to tell her she'd asked Curt to have coffee with her. While she loved Mom, Taylor didn't think she needed to know every single aspect of her life. Unfortunately, living in the same house made it next to impossible to keep many things private. "The night he had dinner here. You'd gone upstairs to check on Reese."

Taylor could practically see the already-spinning wheels in Mom's head go into overdrive.

"Did he ask you?" Both Mom's expression and tone became suspicious.

"Nope." Taylor put her earring in and waited for the next question. Mom wouldn't let her get away with a one-word answer.

Mom crossed her arms and glared at her. "You didn't ask just so you can interrogate him, did you?"

"Of course not. Do you really think I'd stoop so low?" Of course she would, if it meant protecting her family. And while she might have considered doing that before dinner, it wasn't why she'd asked him.

Mom nodded. "Under certain circumstances you wouldn't think twice before doing exactly that, Taylor Walker. But if not so you can give him the third degree, what prompted you to ask him?"

Good question. She hadn't planned on it when he walked in, that's for sure. And while he was very handsome—okay, handsome didn't do the man justice—she didn't ask out every attractive guy she met.

His reaction to Mom's not-so-subtle attempts to leave them alone, and his treatment of Reese made the decision for her. He hadn't shrugged off Reese's personal questions. Instead, he'd answered them. He hadn't seemed annoyed when Reese dominated much of the conversation, either. In her experience, both men and women without children of their own often didn't understand that kids liked to talk and share their day with others. Even when the day's events were uneventful.

Dennis, the last man she dated, was a perfect example of that. After they'd been together for about two months, Mom suggested she invite him over for dinner so she and Reese could get to know him better. Much like she had the night Curt was over, Reese spent a good ten minutes telling them about her day, starting with morning work and ending with Ryan, a boy in her class, tripping and cutting his knee on the way to the bus.

The next time they went out, Dennis let her know what he thought about Reese and children in general. He'd gone on to remind her that Reese was her niece, not her daughter, and not her responsibility. She hadn't bothered to fill him in on the specifics of the situation. Instead, she left his apartment without looking back. They never spoke again after that night.

This afternoon, she might discover Curt was as big a jerk as Dennis. She hoped not.

Rather than go into great detail, she said, "He seemed nice, so I asked him."

Mom started petting Stripes, who let her know he appreciated it by purring. "He's nice to look at, too. And his eyes. I could sit and look at them all day. It's too bad he wears glasses. I wonder if he's ever considered getting contacts. Or maybe laser eye surgery. Lots of people have it done these days."

"Mom, you've got a serious problem," Taylor said, laughing. Her mom had a thing for blue eyes. In fact, Dad used to joke and say Mom only agreed to go out with him because he had blue eyes.

"Don't tell me you didn't notice."

Oh, she'd noticed. And his eyes weren't the only physical characteristic to capture her attention.

***

Curt had spent the last few days filling the dumpster out front with parts from the outdated kitchen. When he wasn't doing demo work he sat in his office, working on his novel. He'd made a lot of progress on both fronts. In another few days he'd have nothing but the old appliances left in the kitchen. Demolishing a room was so much quicker and easier than putting it back together. In terms of the book, he'd added another eight thousand words. If he maintained the same pace, he'd have a first draft completed by the beginning of June, giving him plenty of time for revisions before he sent it off to the editor for her thoughts. She'd have thoughts, too, if her edits and comments on his last book were any indication.

For the next few hours, though, he didn't plan on thinking about either project. They'd both be there when he came home.

A white Chevy Malibu stopped alongside his car before he could do anything more than back out of his driveway. Immediately, Priscilla waved and put down her window. At the same time the back window went down, too, and a small hand waved at him.

"Hi. Mimi and I are going for pizza," Reese said before either adult could exchange a proper greeting.

"Pizza is one of my favorite foods," Curt said.

"You have to go to Luigi's. Their pizza is way better than Dino's. Mimi says Luigi's makes it in a special oven. We're going to Luigi's now."

"Hello, Curt. Trust her; when it comes to either pizza or tacos she knows what she's taking about. Luigi's uses a brick oven for their pizza. They have decent pasta and subs as well. They have a menu on the Internet if you ever want to call for take-out or delivery."

"We're getting ice cream after. I asked Auntie Taylor to come, but she said she was seeing you. Do you want to come? We can go back and get Auntie and all go together."

In the front seat, it looked like Priscilla was trying not to laugh.

"Sounds like a lot of fun. Can I get a rain check?" He didn't want to hurt the girl's feelings.

"What's a rain check?" Reese asked.

"It means can I go with you, your grandmother, and aunt another time." He couldn't recall ever needing to really consider his word choice. Of course, he didn't have many conversations with first-graders either.

"You can have a rain check. But why do they call it a rain check if there's no rain?" Reese asked, sounding confused.

"No idea." He'd never considered it before, but the kid had a good point.

"Mimi, do you know?"

"I'm not sure either. Maybe we can look it up on the computer when we come back."

Since Reese let the matter go, Curt guessed Priscilla's suggestion appeased her curiosity for the moment.

"Enjoy the afternoon," Priscilla said. "We'll see you later."

From the back seat, Reese waved at him again. "Bye," she called before the window went up and they drove away.

When he walked up the steps, he heard a popular country song through the screen door. He didn't recall the name of it, but he'd heard it the last time he visited his cousin and his family. Trent's wife was a big country fan, and she was slowly converting Trent. Before he could ring the bell, Taylor appeared in the hallway, suggesting she'd been watching for him.

"Let me turn off the music, and we can go." She pushed the door open so he could enter. The sunlight streaming through the front windows bounced off the golden highlights in her hair that he'd failed to notice the night he ate dinner with the Walkers.

"I'm in no rush. I spent the morning working."

He followed her with his eyes as she walked away, liking what he saw. When he'd come for dinner, she had on capris and a tank top. Even dressed like that he could tell she took excellent care of herself. Today's outfit revealed even more. The sundress ended several inches above the knee in the front, exposing her long, lean legs. Unfortunately, the back of it hit midcalf. He never understood why women insisted on wearing long dresses, especially when they had great legs. She'd tied her hair up again, but at least her choice of hairstyles meant he got a perfect view of her sun-kissed shoulders and upper back. Considering it was only spring, Taylor had a great tan, suggesting she spent a lot of time outside.

The music stopped and Taylor reappeared, a small purse hanging from her shoulder. "All set."

He hadn't left the house much since moving in. The only places he'd visited had been the grocery store and the hardware store. Except for the day he looked at the house and his GPS took him on a little tour, he hadn't driven around town. He'd seen no real reason to at this point. It wasn't like he planned on becoming a permanent member of the community. So when Taylor suggested they go to the Java Bean, she had to give him directions.

Curt looked at the small café located on Mammoth Road. A handful of cars were parked out front, and a large sign with the words The Java Bean hung over a window, the *B* in the word Bean actually in the shape of a giant coffee bean. A line of cars waited for their turn at the drive-thru window.

"Looks like a popular place." He pulled into an empty spot away from the other vehicles.

"It is, especially when there are games at either the soccer or the baseball fields. Both are just down the street." Taylor opened the door before he managed to get the keys from the ignition, making it impossible for him get it for her, something he normally did for any woman he took out, including his mom.

The scent of apple pie and coffee greeted him the moment he opened the café door. If the smells were anything to go on, he'd be visiting this place a lot while he lived in town. "It all looks delicious. What do you suggest?"

Two long glass cases stood full of every tasty dessert imaginable. Behind the counter on the wall, a long list of coffee blends and specialty drinks was mounted, along with a listing of all the sandwiches available.

"Their pies are unbelievable. I've never had better anywhere, not even in the city. The cookies taste like homemade, and the sandwiches are huge. I can never finish even a small one. During the week, they also serve soup. You should try it sometime." She stepped closer to him. Right away he noticed that a heavy cloud of perfume didn't overwhelm him. His last girlfriend had often smelled as if she took baths in perfume. The smell would linger in his car or apartment for days.

"The only things I don't love are their cakes. They tend to be a little dry," she whispered. "When we need to order one, we go to a bakery in Hudson instead."

He wasn't a big cake person anyway. "What are you having?"

"The mixed berry pie and a coffee." She pointed to a golden-brown pie in the case. "They make it with blueberries, raspberries, boysenberries, and blackberries. There's nothing better than a slice of it warm, with vanilla ice cream on top, and a hot coffee."

"Then we'll make it two slices. If you want to find us a table, I'll order. How do you like your coffee?" Curt asked.

"How about the other way around? I asked you out, which means this is on me."

Two firsts in one week. Although a woman had never asked him out before, when Taylor had his response had been a no-brainer. This was different. "I don't mind getting it." He didn't want to cause a scene, but he didn't want her picking up the tab even if it was only for some pie and coffee.

Two women got in line behind them, but their presence didn't stop Taylor from shaking her head. "I appreciate the offer, but not today." She stepped forward, handed the teenager at the counter a twenty, and then placed their order.

He considered demanding the teen hand the money back and accept his instead. Doing so would cause a scene and draw attention to them. Avoiding unnecessary attention remained number one on his priority list. It would also piss Taylor off. They hadn't spent much time together, but everything he'd seen suggested she was one stubborn woman. Curt was related to enough stubborn people to know, if he kept pushing the matter, she'd only dig in further. He'd prefer to avoid a standoff this afternoon.

"Next time it's on me," he said, picking up the tray the teenager set down. And he planned on there being a next time soon.

"Fair enough," she said, in the silky voice he found so at odds with the little he knew about her.

She selected a table near a tall bookcase packed with books, some of which looked like they'd seen better days. A framed sign on one shelf said: Take A Book, Leave A Book, or Do Both.

"Do you mind if I sit on this side?" She went toward the chair against the wall. Unlike the car door outside, he managed to pull the chair out before she did it herself. Her bluish-gray eyes widened with surprise, telling him no man had ever pulled a chair out for her before. "Thank you." Her voice echoed the emotion. "I don't like my back to the door," she explained after sitting down.

Curt handed over her pie and coffee before taking his off the tray. Already his mouth watered at the sweet smell wafting up from the plate. "Mind if I ask why?" Personally, he didn't care if his back was to a door or not, as long as he had a seat under his ass.

"It's a security thing. I like to know who comes in and goes out. If I can monitor that, it's easier to respond in case of an emergency."

He'd never thought much about it; now that she mentioned it, though, he saw how facing the door could be beneficial. "Makes sense."

"Drives my mom crazy when we go out to a restaurant, but she's used to it. Reese finds it funny, and usually wants to sit next to me."

"Your niece invited me for pizza and ice cream today, right before I picked you up."

Taylor smiled at the mention of Reese. "She loves

people. You could've been with someone she'd never met and she would've invited you both along. Her teachers always tell us she's the most caring student in class."

Us? Did she mean Priscilla and her, or was Reese's mother included in the statement, too? Priscilla had mentioned having another daughter, and he guessed she was Reese's mother. During dinner, though, Reese never mentioned her mom, and it was evident Reese lived with Taylor and Priscilla. Did her mom live there, too? He didn't think so. While it wasn't any of his business, he wondered about their family dynamic.

"We need more people in the world like her," he said before he tasted the pie. Or maybe he should say, tasted something fit for the gods. When Taylor said their pies were unbelievable, she hadn't been kidding. He dug his fork in for more.

"Told you it was incredible."

"I'm going to get a whole pie to take home with me."

Taylor leaned her chin on her hand. "That might not be safe. You might find me climbing through a window in the middle of the night to steal it."

Curt pictured her shimmying her way through a window. In his mind, though, it wasn't the kitchen she found herself in, but his bedroom, and it wasn't pie she was looking for. "No need to sneak in. Just ring the bell and I'll share with you."

He reached for his coffee and forced the erotic images from his head. He'd never been a player like his cousin Trent, but he dated. He'd even been in a few long-term relationships. His last relationship, though, had ended five months ago, and he hadn't been with a woman since.

She snapped her fingers. "Darn it. I should've recorded you saying that in case I show up at ten o'clock tonight, and you've changed your mind. Maybe I'll play it safe and buy one, too." Finally Taylor reached for her fork. "Of course, if I do, I'll need to get at least a slice of chocolate chip pie or some cookies for Reese. She'd never forgive me if I came home with pie for Mom and me but nothing for her."

Her statement confirmed his previous suspicion. Reese's mom didn't live with them.

"She *was* getting ice cream and pizza today," he reminded her.

Taylor smiled, and a dimple appeared in her right cheek. "You don't spend much time around kids, do you?"

Curt thought about his answer before he spoke. "The only children I've been around are my cousins' kids, and they're still young. The oldest will be two in the fall."

"Well, trust me, Reese could've stopped here and had chocolate chip pie after eating ice cream, and she'd still be disappointed if I brought home pie for myself and nothing for her."

They ate in silence for a few seconds before Taylor put down her fork and reached for her coffee. "You mentioned your cousins. Do you have a big family?"

He'd been the one to open his mouth and bring up his family. If he hoped to keep everyone from learning who he really was, he needed to watch his words more carefully. "Oh, yeah. My dad is one of four and my mom is one of seven. I have more first cousins than I can count, and now they're starting to have children."

"One of seven? I hope your mom had more than one bathroom growing up." Taylor laughed, the sound rippling across the table, and he laughed, too. "My sister and I were always fighting over ours. There's only one full bathroom in the house, so we had to share it with our parents, too. Mom had to make a schedule when we were in middle school and high school so we both got ready on time."

Curt thought of the estate his mom grew up on and where his grandparents still lived. "They had more than one." Truthful and to the point. "What about you? Do you have a big family?"

"Average. My mom has a sister and brother. Both live nearby. My dad had two sisters. One lives in town, and the other moved to Arizona a few years ago. My cousins are spread throughout New England."

"Do you only have one sister?"

Taylor's eyes grew sad, and she reached for her fork again. "Yes. Eliza is a year older than me. You'd think since we're so close in age we would've had a lot in common, but we've always been complete opposites."

He knew all about that. "I've never had a lot in common with my brother, either. I'd do anything for him and he's the same way, but it's hard to believe we have the same parents. I have more in common with my sister."

"Family can be complicated." She shook her head ever so slightly. "Let's talk about something other than family."

Curt had no complaints there.

They discussed her work with the DEA while they finished their pie and first cups of coffee. Then, he answered her questions about why he'd become a writer and where he got his ideas. Unwilling to end their time together, he bought them another round of coffee. He also purchased a whole mixed berry pie to take home with him.

"I noticed the dumpster outside the house when I went running this week."

"Started tearing apart the kitchen this week. It seemed like the best place to remodel first," Curt answered. "I can't grill outside forever."

She nodded in agreement. "Are you really going to do it all yourself? It's been a while since I've been inside the house, but it seems like a lot of work for one person."

"I'm going to try. I have a friend I can call if I need some help." He'd met Ed in the first carpentry class he'd taken. At the time the older man had been approaching retirement, and his wife wanted him to have a hobby so he didn't sit at home all day driving her crazy. Despite the age gap, they'd hit it off. Ed had helped him more than once on projects. "And I can always call you, right? Priscilla said you worked alongside your father."

"My dad did teach me a thing or two about hammering

a nail. I guess I could help if you get into a jam. But it'll cost you."

"Name your price."

"Mmm." She tapped her fingers against the tabletop. Today her nails were painted a dark purple. "I'll need to think about it and get back to you."

"How about we start with dinner some night this week?" He would've said tomorrow, but he'd already made plans with his cousin.

The corner of Taylor's mouth inched upward. "Weeknights can be tricky. Things come up sometimes. Like last night, I didn't get home until well after midnight. I even ended up having to skip Reese's soccer game today."

Her job might be essential, but it sounded terrible. "How about next Saturday night, then?" A week would give him plenty of time to scout out a nice place to take her. He knew plenty of five-star restaurants in and around Boston, but he'd prefer to avoid them all, for numerous reasons.

"I'll pencil you in for next weekend."

CHAPTER FOUR

Taylor tried to steal the ball as Reese dribbled it across the backyard Sunday afternoon. Before she could intercept it, though, her niece kicked it toward the goal. She missed, and the ball rolled past the goal and toward the woods.

"I'll get it," Reese called out, sprinting after the runaway soccer ball.

"While you do, I'm going to take a water break." They'd been out there for at least an hour. Reese didn't look even close to tiring out. The child had an endless supply of energy.

When they'd come out, she'd left two bottles of water on the patio table. Opening one, she took a long swallow, the cool drink immediately perking her up. A few feet away, her mom checked on the chicken and burgers she'd put on the grill. The house had no central air conditioning, only window units, so once the weather turned warmer they cooked outside as much as possible to keep the inside temperature down.

"Maybe we should see if Curt wants to join us." Priscilla closed the grill cover and took a seat at the table. "We have plenty of food."

This was the first time Mom had mentioned Curt since

their conversation early yesterday afternoon. She'd expected a million questions as soon as she came home from having coffee with him. Oddly, Mom never said a word except a thank-you for bringing home the pie. She should've known that was too good to last.

"He has plans today." He hadn't given her any particular details and, it being none of her business, she hadn't asked.

"C'mon, Auntie. I got the ball." Reese walked past the goal, carrying the pink-and-white soccer ball in her hands.

Just what she thought; Reese wasn't ready to quit for the afternoon.

"Why don't you practice by yourself for a little bit and give Aunt Taylor a break," Mom suggested. "I think you wore her out."

Yep, the reprieve from questioning was over. Mom planned to start her interrogation now.

Reese shrugged and dropped the ball to the ground. "Okay."

Having no siblings or friends next door, Reese was used to playing alone. She dribbled the ball across the yard toward the goal, leaving Taylor alone with Mom.

"Go ahead and ask away," Taylor said. Mom had questions. The sooner she asked, the sooner they could talk about something else.

"Can you blame me for being curious?" Mom asked.

Blame her? No, not really. Wish she'd mind her own business on this? Yes, most certainly.

"Considering you only went for coffee at the Java Bean, you were gone for a long time yesterday." Mom refilled her iced tea from the pitcher she'd brought outside earlier. "I assume that means he's not a serial killer who runs around at night wearing a clown costume."

The statement rubbed her the wrong way. "Mom, I didn't interrogate him. We just talked." They'd talked so much they'd both lost track of time as one coffee turned into another. In the end, they'd each had three cups.

"Relax. I'm kidding. I'm glad you enjoyed yourself." She paused with her glass almost to her lips. "You did enjoy yourself, right?"

Definitely. She found talking with Curt easy. They'd discussed a huge range of topics. They'd even touched on politics a little, something she tended to avoid with most people. She found too many people got upset when you didn't share the same political views as them. Often, those same people tried to convert you to their way of thinking. Rather than risk a disagreement or offend someone, she was selective about with whom she discussed the topic. While she and Curt shared some of the same political views, they hadn't agreed on everything. Much to his credit, he hadn't insisted his opinion was correct or tried to convert her to his way of thinking.

Not only was Curt easy to talk to, but there was also something about him. Something that set him apart from the men she'd gone out with before. She'd first noticed when he insisted on paying for coffee. He hadn't argued with her, but it had been obvious it didn't sit well with him. Dennis had never had a problem when she paid. A few times, he even suggested they split a bill.

Curt pulling out her chair, and later opening the car door for her, stood out vividly in her head. Dad used to open doors all the time for Mom, but he was from a different generation. Men didn't do things like that anymore. At least, she'd never met any who did. Yet Curt had done both, and not because he was trying to impress her. No, it'd been too automatic on his part. Like it'd been ingrained in him to treat a woman a certain way.

"I did."

"And will there be a second date?"

"It wasn't a date, Mom. We talked and drank coffee." Jeez, why did she keep insisting it was a date?

"Okay. Then, will there be a first date?" She set down her tea and moved back to the grill to check on the food.

"Next weekend."

"Oh, how exciting. Now aren't you glad I invited him over after he brought Stripes home?"

If she said yes, heaven knew how many other guys Mom might start inviting over for dinner. "Maybe a little, but let's not make a habit of inviting men to dinner. I prefer finding my own dates, Mom. Okay?"

Mom looked over her shoulder, a smile stretched across her face. Whatever she intended to say, Taylor wasn't going to appreciate. "Who knows? Maybe he'll be the one." She turned her attention back to the chicken. "He's polite, successful, and he appeared comfortable interacting with Reese. So far, everything points toward him being a keeper."

There Mom went with her romantic fantasies again. "You're getting ahead of yourself. We had pie and coffee. That's it. Before you reserve the church and call the photographer, let us go out again."

"Fine, fine. I'll wait until next week to call Reverend Shawn."

"Why are you calling Reverend Shawn?" Reese asked, stopping for a water break just in time to catch her grandmother's statement.

Taylor threw her mom a look that said, "nice going— you answer this one."

"Grown-up stuff," Mom said. "Nothing to worry about. Dinner is almost done. Why don't you go inside and wash your hands?"

"Please tell me, Mimi." The girl didn't like to be left out of anything. "Why are you calling Reverend Shawn?"

Taylor watched Mom struggle with an answer Reese would accept. "I want to see if the church needs extra help for this year's Old Home Day."

Every year the church sponsored the town's Old Home Day celebration, an event that had started in 1906 and grown over the years. Today, the entire town got involved with it.

Satisfied with the answer, Reese dropped her soccer

ball into the bucket of outside toys on the patio, and went inside.

"She hears everything," Mom said. "Before she comes back, is there anything else you'd care to share about our handsome new neighbor?"

"He's different. But not in a bad way or anything." Taylor thought for a good way to describe what she meant. "It sounds cheesy, but I'd use the word classy to describe him. He pulls out chairs, opens doors."

"There are much worse things a person can be."

She agreed with that.

Mom put the platter of hamburgers and chicken on the table. They'd already brought out a garden salad and potato chips. "There's something about him that seems familiar. I can't put my finger on what it is."

Taylor tore open the chips and uncovered the salad bowl. "He probably reminds you of someone you've seen on a television show or in a movie."

"I'm sure you're right," Mom agreed, dropping the matter.

***

In Curt's opinion, a long motorcycle ride was a damn good way to spend a gorgeous spring afternoon. He'd left his house over two hours ago, sticking to the back roads as much as possible. The highway would've shaved at least forty minutes from the drive, maybe even more, but who wanted to be stuck on the highway when it was this nice out? Definitely not him.

After parking in the underground garage, Curt took the stairs up to the Hillcrest's main lobby. Both his cousins Trent and Gray lived in the exclusive downtown Providence complex. He'd visited both on numerous occasions, and never before had a problem going right on up without first stopping at the security desk. Today, as he walked toward one of the two public elevators, a uniformed security guard stopped him.

"Excuse me. All guests must check in before going

upstairs," the guard said. "Who are you here to see today?"

He remembered Dion, the security guard on duty, from his many previous visits; obviously the guard didn't recognize him. "I'm visiting Gray Sherbrooke. He's expecting me, Dion."

"I'll need to call up and verify. Name, please." The guard picked up the phone and waited for an answer.

If nothing else, this further assured him his close-trimmed beard and longer hair helped conceal his identity. "Curt Sherbrooke." He pulled his ID from his wallet and handed it over.

The guard glanced at it and then took a good look at him. "So sorry, Mr. Sherbrooke. I didn't recognize you. It's good to see you again." Dion handed the ID back and put down the phone. "Go on up. Have a nice afternoon."

Curt rode the elevator up with two women, both definite head-turners. They were dressed in the latest spring styles, their makeup and hair perfect.

The taller of the two kept looking his way and smiling, her interest in him obvious. Any other day he would've asked for a phone number. Today he smiled back, but otherwise kept to himself.

"I'm Linda. I just moved in last month," she said as the elevator passed the fourth floor. "This is my sister, Katie." She gestured to the other woman. "Do you live here, or are you visiting?"

"Just visiting. I'm sure you'll enjoy living here; my cousin, Gray, and his fiancée do."

"I live a floor below Gray and Kiera. If he's your cousin, you must be a Sherbrooke. Don't tell me. Let me guess." She paused, and he imagined her running through a list of his family members. "You're definitely not Scott or Jake." Linda smiled and pointed at him. "Curt, right?"

"Correct." *Come on, elevator, reach her floor already.*

Linda pulled a business card and pen from her purse. "Here's my cell number if you want to give me a call sometime," she said as she wrote on the blank side of the card.

The elevator door opened, and he wondered how he could decline without offending her. In the end, he didn't have to worry about it because she pressed the card into his hand and walked away with her sister, the doors closing behind them.

Curt flipped the card over. *Linda Hurley, Attorney at Law* was printed on the front, along with Hale & Associates. The name of the same downtown law firm his cousin Derek and his wife, Brooklyn, worked for. He shoved the card into his back pocket. Later it'd find its way into the trash. His instincts told him Linda Hurley wasn't his type anyway. She reminded him too much of his last girlfriend—unlike the DEA agent living next door to him. When it came to Taylor, his instincts told him something altogether different.

"Holy hell," Gray said in lieu of a greeting when he opened the apartment door moments later. "Do they not have mirrors where you live?"

In many ways Curt was closer to Gray than his own brother. They were about a year apart in age and shared many of the same interests. Of course, that meant Gray felt no qualms about busting Curt's balls every chance he got.

"Aunt Judith said you'd moved to New Hampshire. I didn't know you'd decided to turn into a tree-hugging wilderness nut. What's next, a plaid flannel shirt?"

Curt ignored Gray's comments and walked inside. The entire apartment smelled like fresh herbs and something delicious he couldn't identify. "Kiera cooking?"

Kiera, Gray's fiancée, was a professionally trained chef who worked at Providence's top French restaurant. More times than not she was in the kitchen, experimenting on a new dish. And if one was lucky enough to be around, they got to enjoy her efforts.

"She was earlier. Now she's getting ready to go out." Gray closed the door and headed for the living room.

"She, Addie, and Brooklyn are going to a concert. Some boy band they all loved in high school is performing. Since he's alone too, Trent's going to come down with Kendrick. I invited Derek over too, but he has other plans."

He hadn't seen Trent in months. It'd be nice to catch up with him.

"What's up with the wild-man look?" Gray asked as his fiancée entered the room.

Kiera immediately bypassed Gray and hugged him instead. Both her parents worked at Uncle Mark's estate, so they'd known each other a long time. "Ignore him, Curt. I think the barely there beard makes you look sexy."

"Linda on the elevator did, too. She gave me her number and told me to call her."

Gray tugged Kiera down next to him. "You're engaged, remember?"

Curt, as well as Kiera, knew Gray was only giving her a hard time.

She elbowed Gray in the side. "That doesn't mean I'm blind, Mr. Sherbrooke." She patted his cousin's cheek. "Don't worry, I find you sexy, too," she said, using a tone one might when placating a small child. "So, who's Linda? And what's up with the new look?"

"She's someone I just met on the elevator. Said she moved in recently. Here's her card if you want to call her." Curt dropped the business card onto the end table. "I don't need it."

"Oh, *that* Linda," Gray said, earning him a cold stare from Kiera.

"Engaged, remember?" she said teasingly.

"And I'll show you just how happily engaged when you come home tonight." Gray kissed Kiera as if Curt wasn't sitting right across from them.

"Hey, I'm still sitting here, remember? Save it for when you're alone, please."

Neither Gray nor Kiera looked the least embarrassed when they pulled apart.

"I'm going. Brooklyn and Addie are waiting for me upstairs. Behave yourselves tonight." While Gray lived in one of the building's three-bedroom apartments, his older brother, Trent, resided in the building's penthouse, which encompassed the top two floors.

"Have fun. Say hi to Addie and Brooklyn." Gray kissed Kiera again before she exited the room.

Left alone, Gray picked up the business card. "You're sure you don't want this?"

Curt nodded before going in search of whatever delicious dish Kiera had cooked up.

"Grab some plates and I'll get the food." Gray followed Curt into the kitchen and went straight for one of the two ovens. "You're not interested in Linda, so are you and Miranda back on?"

He'd started seeing Miranda Bergman sometime the previous summer. He'd even taken her to his cousin's wedding in September. He'd ended their relationship in December, though. "Nope. Derek told me she's with his buddy, Colton Horne. Hope it works out for them. They seem well suited."

Although sweet as well as beautiful, Miranda loved the spotlight, which was one of the main reasons he'd stopped seeing her. While Miranda wanted everyone to notice her, he preferred to fly low and not draw any extra attention to himself. Colton, on the other hand, shared Miranda's need for attention. Anyone who'd ever met the guy would agree.

"There'd better be some of whatever Kiera cooked left." Trent's voice announced his arrival.

"Did you forget how to knock?" Gray called out.

"I ran into Kiera. She told me to let myself in."

Trent entered the kitchen, his eleven-month-old son in his arms and a large diaper bag hanging from his shoulder. Curt couldn't help but laugh at the sight of his once-carefree playboy cousin so domesticated. Of all his cousins, Trent had been the last one he expected to ever marry and have a family.

"What the—" Trent caught himself before he said something he shouldn't in front of his son. "What happened to you?"

"He's going for the *Left in the Wild* look," Gray answered, referring to a popular reality show where they dumped four couples somewhere remote and they had to survive for a month on their own.

He'd brushed off Gray's teasing before, but now it was starting to get to him. "Both of you can stuff it." He'd prefer much more colorful language, but he had to watch it with Kendrick in the room. Trent's wife would kill him if the baby started repeating any four-letter words he might overhear.

"He moved to New Hampshire and decided to become one with nature," Gray said while he filled three plates with whatever dish he'd pulled from the oven.

"You moved way up there?" Trent asked. "Why?"

Curt nodded. "The town isn't far up. I can be in Massachusetts in about ten or fifteen minutes."

Trent put Kendrick down, and immediately the baby toddled over to his uncle.

"He's walking already?" Curt asked. When he'd last seen Kendrick, he'd only been crawling.

"Started last month. It's a whole new level of craziness at home now," Trent answered, dropping the diaper bag onto the floor.

"I think he's having an identity crisis," Gray said, going back to busting Curt's ass again. "He even turned down the phone number of a beautiful woman. Linda Hurley gave him her card, and he told me to toss it."

Curt took the dish his cousin offered and wondered why he'd thought spending an evening with Gray was a good idea. Instead, he could be home writing or, even better, having dinner with his single next-door neighbor. "No kind of crisis. Just trying to go unnoticed while I'm living in Pelham. I don't need the distractions while I finish the book and work on the house."

"Another renovation project. What's this, your fourth?" Trent asked. "Is this one similar to the house in Marlborough?"

"Bigger, older, and it needs more work. Since I've left Nichols Investment, I decided to live in the house while I renovate it. Makes it easier. After it's done I'll move back to Boston. I kept my condo there."

"I'd offer to help, but you wouldn't want it." Trent picked up Kendrick and sat him on his lap. "I see the long hair and the beard's a disguise. Wish I'd considered that in the past. I certainly could've used it."

Prior to his marriage, Trent had graced more tabloid magazine covers and Internet sites than anyone Curt knew. No easy feat when you're part of the Sherbrooke family. There had been a point where the guy couldn't even enjoy a coffee without someone snapping a picture of him and selling it to the highest bidder.

"Is it working?" Trent asked, while he tried to keep his son from reaching for the food on the plate.

"Yeah, so far." Curt thought of his neighbors and cringed. "More or less, anyway."

"Either a disguise works or it doesn't." Gray put his own plate down on the kitchen island, then went back to the refrigerator. When he came back he carried a container of baby strawberry yogurt and a baby-sized spoon. "Kiera got Kendrick's favorite at the store." He passed the spoon and yogurt to Trent. "Which is it, Curt?"

"I've only met the women who live next door. The three of them know I'm an author, but that's it."

Next to him Trent fed his son the yogurt, but the baby kept eyeing the food on his father's plate instead. Curt didn't blame the kid. Given the choice between strawberry yogurt and the roasted chicken Provençal Kiera had prepared, he wouldn't want the yogurt either.

"Three women living next door. Is one of them the reason you're not interested in Linda's number?" Gray asked, his eyebrow cocked knowingly.

"Linda reminds me of Miranda. You know why I ended it with her," Curt offered as an answer.

"Can't disagree with you on that one. I've only run into Linda a few times, but I get the same impression. Derek would know better. He works with her." Gray walked away again and returned with three bottles of sparkling water. "But Linda would provide a little distraction. You've got to do something besides hide out up there in New Hampshire. Or is one of your new neighbors providing you with that?"

"Yeah, but not in the way you mean." *At least not yet.* "Yesterday Taylor and I went for coffee. Saturday, I'm taking her for dinner."

"But she doesn't know who you are?" Trent set aside the yogurt container and started on his own meal.

"Like I said, Taylor and her mom, Priscilla, know I'm C.S. Hilton. Besides, we're only going for dinner." He didn't look at either of his cousins when he answered.

Gray narrowed his eyes and looked at him. "She lives with her mother. Exactly how old is she?"

"Don't go there. She's a DEA agent in Boston. She lives next door with her mother and niece. I don't know the specifics, but Reese's mom isn't around. Taylor and Priscilla are bringing her up."

Trent laughed. "You're going to take a federal agent out for dinner and not tell her who you are? You realize she might figure it out, right? Investigating is part of her job."

"He's right," Gray agreed with a shake of his head. "Can't believe I just said that."

"She believes I'm Curt Hilton, an author from Boston who likes to renovate old houses. Why would she investigate anything?"

"And what happens if you decide you want more than one dinner out, dude?" Gray asked, bringing up something Curt had already considered.

Trent gave up trying to keep Kendrick from sampling

his roasted chicken, and raised his fork containing the tiniest amount toward the baby's mouth. "You're asking for trouble. Take my word for it, women don't like secrets."

"Damn it. I have to agree with Trent again." Gray sounded disgusted. "And secrets have a way of coming out. Much better to be up-front with her now. Either that or avoid your neighbors altogether, if you really want them to believe you're Curt Hilton."

Taylor intrigued him too much to stay away. And he saw no reason she'd suspect he was anything more than he told her. "Trust me, it's no big deal. Everything'll be fine."

Both Gray and Trent laughed knowingly. "Famous last words if I ever heard 'em," Trent said with a smirk.

Gray smiled and shared his comment, too. "Yep. Make sure you let us know when it blows up in your face."

CHAPTER FIVE

He'd done his research. According to the Internet, Pellegrino in Windham was the perfect restaurant for tonight. It offered a diverse Italian menu, was several notches above the average chain restaurant, but at the same time it wasn't so expensive the prices would raise any questions in Taylor's mind. Questions that might kick her into investigator mode. Thanks to his cousins and their comments, he kept remembering what she did for a living. If she went there, it wouldn't be too difficult for her to learn the truth. His full legal name was on record as the owner of the house. It would be easy enough to visit the town hall and obtain the information.

Wednesday night, he considered coming clean with Taylor and her mom. They'd invited him over for dinner again and he'd accepted. After spending three days alone in his house, he'd appreciated the chance for human contact. Much like on his first visit, Reese gave them the 411 on her day at school. Once she stopped talking long enough to put some food in her mouth, Priscilla told him about some of the upcoming events in town. Apparently, starting in the spring, a farmers' market was set up every Wednesday on the village green, and one could find everything from local honey to unique cheeses for sale there. The town also held several free concerts on the village green in the summer. In July the town sponsored a fireworks display, although Priscilla did say a lot of residents did their own. She'd made a point to remind him of the town's Old Home Day celebration at the end of the summer. He had no idea what it was, but he got the impression it was a big deal in Pelham. Once she filled him in on everything the town offered, she asked about his progress on the house. That had taken them through the rest of dinner. Afterward, he returned home and again told himself it didn't matter at this point. If somehow things between him and Taylor developed past a casual relationship, he'd come clean. No need to rush anything.

Since then, he'd only seen Taylor once. Unable to sleep, he'd started work early Friday morning. He'd been carrying scraps from the kitchen out to the rented dumpster when Taylor jogged past. She'd mentioned often running in the morning, but this had been the first time he'd seen her. She'd been dressed in running shorts and a sports bra. Like he'd already guessed, she had a knockout body. Lean and toned, she had great muscle definition, but didn't look like she spent every waking hour either in the gym or counting each calorie she put in her mouth. His last girlfriend had lived on lettuce and water. She'd spent crazy hours on a treadmill or in either a Pilates or yoga class. He'd hated taking Miranda out to eat. She'd order something small off the menu, then sit there and look at it while he enjoyed whatever meal he got. Standing next to her, he'd felt like he was with a paper doll who might fly away if the wind blew.

Curt didn't need to worry about Taylor flying away. He'd also seen her eat. While not an overeater, at least the times he'd been around, she had a healthy appetite. She even indulged in dessert, if their coffee date was anything to go by. She'd not only polished off a large slice of pie, but had brought an entire one home with her to share with

Priscilla. He'd taken one home, too. It had lasted one day. He'd considered going back for another several times since then. Depending on how things progressed tonight, they could meet up tomorrow and grab some pie for breakfast.

What happens if you decide you want more than one dinner out, dude? Women don't like secrets. Curt pictured Gray and Trent saying the words as he grabbed his car keys off his nightstand.

"Go with it for now." He put on the glasses he'd adopted since moving.

He reached the end of the hall before he caught his reflection in the huge antique mirror hanging on the wall. He hadn't decided yet if he wanted to keep it or not, and since it wasn't in his way he'd asked the cleaning crew to leave it. Tonight, he almost didn't recognize the person in the glass. He should've anticipated his cousins' reactions over the weekend. He'd always been anal about getting his hair cut. His hair grew like a weed on steroids, so he had a standing appointment once a month with his stylist in Boston. If the stylist saw his hair now, the poor man would keel over in his salon chair. The beard, though, was what really made the difference. He'd started shaving at fourteen, and had never gone for more than a few days without doing so since. Honestly, he'd had his cousin Scott in mind when he started letting his grow in. Scott had favored a well-trimmed beard for a few years. It looked good on Scott. On him, the jury was still out.

Stripes was stretched out on the top step, soaking up all the early evening sun he could. When Curt approached, the cat looked up, swished his tail back and forth, and then went back to enjoying the sun, dismissing Curt entirely. Taking the feline's cue, he ignored the cat and rang the Walkers' doorbell.

A stampede of unseen elephants ran toward the door. At least it sounded like a whole herd of them coming, but an elephant didn't open the door. Instead, a petite almost-seven-year-old wearing a soccer T-shirt and shorts and with dirt on her face did.

"Hi, you're here to get Auntie Taylor." Reese pushed the screen door open, a bright welcoming smile on her face. The sound of the door got Stripes' attention, and he jumped to his feet, slipping inside while he could. "Auntie Taylor, Curt's here!" Reese shouted up the stairs once Curt came inside. "Auntie's upstairs fixing her hair. And Mimi is in the kitchen. C'mon." She took him by the wrist, leaving him no option but to follow her down the short hallway. "Mimi, Curt's here," she announced, as if Priscilla hadn't already heard the girl shout upstairs.

"So I heard." She handed her granddaughter a colorful cup with cats on it as Reese passed by. "Can I get you anything? Taylor should be down in a minute. We got stuck in traffic on the way home from Reese's soccer game."

"Have some of Mimi's sweet tea, it's the best. Way better than the stuff at Peggy Sue's."

He'd passed a restaurant named Peggy Sue's when he'd gone shopping for kitchen flooring yesterday. He hadn't stopped inside, but from the exterior it looked like a well-preserved 1950s diner. "Well, if Reese says it's the best, I'd better try some," Curt answered.

Priscilla poured him a glass before pouring one for herself. "My mom grew up in Tennessee, and moved north after she got married. People up here don't know the proper way of making sweet tea. They think all you need to do is add some sugar."

Both Priscilla and Reese watched him as he took his first sip. It turned into several more before he put the glass down. "I have to agree with Reese."

Reese gave him another full-mouth grin.

"Did you win your game today?" he asked.

She nodded, her long ponytail moving back and forth. "Yup. We've only lost one game all spring. I played in the winter, too, but my team wasn't as good."

"That happens. When I played lacrosse, sometimes we

had a great team and sometimes we didn't.'"

"I want to try lacrosse, but Auntie Taylor and Mimi said I can't do both because the games are both on the weekends. Did you ever play soccer?"

For a girl who wasn't even seven, Reese seemed able to carry on good conversations. Or maybe all kids her age could. "No, I played football and lacrosse. My older brother tried soccer, but liked hockey better."

Reese considered his answer while she enjoyed her tea. "If you want, I can teach you. I'm really good."

Priscilla came up behind Reese's chair. She gave him a look that said "I'm sorry." "Curt's probably too busy right now, sweetie. He's got that whole house to work on."

"Oh." The girl's smile vanished.

"Maybe one weekend you can give me a lesson." He hated the disappointment on the kid's face, and what was an hour or so?

Reese's smile returned immediately.

Make sure you let us know when it blows up in your face. He remembered Gray's final comment before they'd changed the subject entirely Sunday night.

Taylor picked what she considered the nicest dress in her closet. Not much of a shopper, her choices for the night were limited to a handful of sundresses, and this outfit, which she'd bought a while ago. Even if the dress was a year old, it'd be fine for their destination tonight. The previous spring she'd attended a friend's bridal shower at Pellegrino wearing this very outfit. She paired it with the open-toed heels that matched, shoes she hadn't worn since the last time she put on the dress. Actually, she hadn't worn heels in months. Generally, the only time she dug them out was when she had to make an appearance in court for a case. Tonight, before heading down, she walked across her bedroom a few times, getting the hang of walking in them again.

Taylor stopped at the kitchen doorway in time to hear

Curt say, "Maybe one weekend you can give me a lesson."

He had his back to her, but she saw the big smile spread across her niece's face. He might not have spent time around kids Reese's age, but he was damn good with her. She'd noticed that on both occasions he'd had dinner with them. What she heard now was further proof.

"And if you want, and it's okay with your grandmother, I'll give you a lesson or two in lacrosse."

Reese had bugged them about trying lacrosse this spring. They hadn't told her no, but rather made her decide between it and soccer because the two conflicted. As expected, Reese stayed with soccer. She'd started playing in preschool and loved it.

Excitement filled her niece's face. "Please, Mimi? Can he?"

"If Curt wants to give you a few lessons, it's fine with me. But no bugging him about it. He'll let you know when he has the time," Mom answered.

Taylor wouldn't put it past Reese to ask him about it every time she saw him. "Mimi's right. You can't nag him about it."

Hearing Taylor's voice, Reese switched her attention from her grandmother to her aunt. "Auntie Taylor, you look so beautiful."

Beautiful might be stretching it, but she appreciated Reese's compliment.

Curt stood and turned when Reese spoke. "She's right." His voice sent a ripple of sensual excitement up her spine. A sensation she hadn't experienced in a long time.

"Thank you." She couldn't recall the last guy to tell her something like that. Should she return the compliment? It wouldn't be a lie if she did, although perhaps beautiful was the wrong adjective. Dressed in khaki-colored pants and a crisp white button-down shirt, he personified sexy.

"Auntie Taylor, I'm goin' to teach Curt how to play soccer, and he's goin' to teach me lacrosse," Reese explained excitedly.

"So I heard. Sounds like a fair trade to me."

"Auntie Taylor taught me how to play. Maybe she can help me and then you can teach her lacrosse, too."

Taylor wouldn't mind getting some one-on-one lessons from Curt, but not in lacrosse.

"If she's interested, I'll give her some lessons too." Curt's already-sensual voice took on an undertone, one that said his thoughts ran in the same direction as Taylor's, and she met his gaze. The interest reflected in his incredible blue eyes confirmed her suspicion.

"When can we start?" Reese asked. "Tomorrow?" Reese, like most kids her age, wasn't one for patience.

"Maybe," Curt answered before either Taylor or Mom could say a word. "If not tomorrow, soon. Promise."

No doubt about it, the guy sure knew how to handle her niece. "I'm ready to leave when you are." She didn't know where the night would end up, but she was eager to get it started.

"Can I come?" Reese asked.

Taylor didn't date often, but men had picked her up at home before. Reese had never before asked to come along. It looked like her niece shared her interest in Curt. And interest put it mildly. He'd captured her attention and refused to give it back. Countless times since their last outing, he'd popped into her thoughts, sometimes at the most inconvenient times.

"Not tonight. Besides, you and Mimi have plans, remember? You're going shopping for Hazel's birthday present."

Reese pouted, but didn't beg to come along. "Will you come check on me when you come home?"

"Always do."

Outside, Curt opened the passenger door before she could touch the handle. He waited until she sat down before closing the door and walking around the front of SUV. *Yup, he's definitely classy.*

He started the vehicle and backed down the long

driveway.

"Do you need directions?" she asked. He hadn't lived in the area long, and he'd admitted he hadn't explored much since moving.

"No need. I got it."

Looked like even classy guys didn't like to get directions when they drove. If he got lost it wouldn't be her fault.

She'd never visited Italy, so she had no firsthand knowledge to go on, but the inside of Pellegrino made her feel as if she'd stepped inside a Tuscan restaurant. Everything from the wall color to the furniture and fireplace had been well thought out to transport customers away for a short while.

The hostess led them to a table for two. A single candle burned, and a small dish filled with olive oil for dipping bread sat in the center.

Like he had at the Java Bean, Curt pulled the chair out for her. In either a coincidence or because he remembered her preference, he gave her the seat facing the main entrance.

"These are our dinner menus." The hostess handed them each a large leather menu. "And this is our wine menu." She placed the third menu near the table's edge. "Your server will be right over."

"I'm not sure what I'm in the mood for tonight." Curt opened the menu, but his attention remained on her. "What about you? Any thoughts?"

Maybe you. Taylor opened her own menu, glad that mind reading was impossible, considering her current thoughts. "Maybe a pasta dish. The last time I ate here, they served beef brasato. It was delicious, but I'd like to try something else."

They both spent several minutes looking over the menu. Pellegrino offered traditional Italian dishes from each region of the country, so there was no shortage of options. Only after they'd ordered wine, something Curt picked out, and their entrees, did she start a conversation.

"For someone who doesn't spend time around children, you're great with them. You made Reese's day. She'll probably plan out a whole soccer training program for you tonight when she gets home."

"She makes it easy."

"Easy and Reese are not words I always associate with each other," she said with a smile. "When we told her someone bought the Cranston house, she hoped some children her age would move in. She gets lonely sometimes, and we can't always drive her over to a friend's house."

"I'm sorry to disappoint her."

"After your promise tonight to let her teach you soccer, I think she's glad you moved in next door." Her niece wasn't the only one pleased he'd moved in, either.

Some emotion passed across his eyes, and he shifted in his seat. "I'll make sure she gets her first lesson in soon."

***

No matter how many five-star reviews a restaurant received, there was always a chance the food wouldn't live up. Tonight, though, the reviews he'd read about Pellegrino proved accurate. The tagliata had been authentic and the service superb. The desserts and after-dinner drinks set in front of them now looked just as fabulous.

He watched Taylor's lips close around her fork, the sight oddly erotic. He had no plans for them after dinner, but he liked the idea of taking her back to his house. Usually Curt could read the women he took out and know if they expected an invite back to his place. Some even made it easy and did the inviting themselves. Taylor wasn't as easy to read. Sometimes she looked at him as if she wanted to tear his clothes off and have sex on the table. Other times her expression said she was enjoying herself, but not looking for anything extra tonight.

"Mmm, this is so good. Wait until you try it," Taylor said, and he forced his eyes away from her mouth.

They'd both ordered tiramisu for dessert, but while he'd gone for an espresso, she'd chosen a latte. "Better than the mixed berry pie last weekend?" He hadn't touched his yet.

"Not better, just different."

He picked up his fork and her eyes followed his movements as he took a taste.

"Well?" Taylor asked.

"It's good, but I think I'll need to try the pie again before I give you a definitive answer on which is better."

"How about I bring one over tomorrow after I drop Reese off at her friend's birthday party?"

They'd spent a fair part of dinner discussing his plans for his kitchen. She'd shared some personal information about herself, too, but she hadn't mentioned the how and why of Reese living with her and Priscilla. He'd kept his mouth closed on the matter. The more personal questions he asked, the more likely she'd do the same. Vague answers like he came from a big family and had two siblings would only fly for so long, especially with Taylor. Eventually she'd expect more specifics. If and when he did share his full identity, he didn't want to do it in a crowded restaurant.

She didn't give him a chance to answer her question about bringing over pie. "What's wrong?" Taylor asked, setting down her fork.

He parted his lips, an answer prepared, but she spoke again.

"And please do *not* say nothing. I read people's facial expressions all the time, so I'm pretty good at it. If you don't want me to come by, you can say it. I won't be offended."

So much for his intended response. "You can come by anytime. Pie or no pie." He reached over and entwined his fingers with hers. "When you mentioned Reese, I wondered if asking why she lived with you and not her parents would be appropriate or not."

67

She pressed her lips together. "You can ask me anything." She sounded weary. "And the reason Reese lives with me and Mom is no big secret."

CHAPTER SIX

"Eliza, my older sister, is Reese's mom. I think I told you we've always been opposites." Taylor pushed her dessert away, even though much of it remained. Since she'd raved about how tasty it was, Curt took that as a sign this was a difficult topic for her. "I never understood how we could be so different. We have the same parents. And they gave us the same opportunities."

Considering how different he and his older brother, Brett, were, this was a topic he could understand. "I've thought the same thing about me and my older brother. Personalities play a big role in the choices we make."

"My dad was a cop in town, but that didn't stop Eliza from getting into the drug scene in high school. At least that's when she said it started. I know she started drinking alcohol in middle school. She went to UNH for a year, but after freshman year she dropped out. She'd failed every course anyway. She bounced from job to job and guy to guy for a few years. Whenever she needed money, she'd show up at our parents' house. They always gave it to her."

Considering the story so far, Curt wondered if her sister had passed away. Drugs claimed a lot of lives, and it would explain why Reese lived with them and not her mother.

"When Eliza got pregnant, we hoped she'd finally get clean. Mom and Dad got her into rehab. When she got out, she moved in with them until Reese was born. We all thought she was finally on the right path. That she'd stay off drugs for her daughter. Get her life together."

He heard the bitterness in her voice.

"About two months after Reese was born, Eliza moved out. She took Reese with her but she'd drop Reese off with Mom several days a week, and often with me on the weekends. She always claimed she had to work. I didn't believe her, and deep down I don't think Mom did either." Taylor paused and took a sip of her latte. "When Reese was seven months old, Eliza's boyfriend at the time and one of his friends decided to hold up a convenience store. Eliza didn't go into the store, but she drove the car. She was arrested and sent to prison, too. Thankfully, no one was hurt. She would've gotten a much longer sentence if they'd shot the clerk working that night."

He wished he'd never asked about Reese's mother.

"I became Reese's legal guardian after that. My sister giving me custody might be the only smart thing she ever did. I think deep down she knew she could never give Reese what she needed, regardless of whether she was in prison or not. Because my hours are sometimes crazy, I moved back in with my mom. Dad passed away a few months before Eliza was arrested, so I think it was good for Mom to have us there."

He couldn't imagine finding himself in a similar situation. "What about Reese's father? Didn't he want custody?"

"Eliza doesn't know who Reese's father is. Considering the men my sister spent time with, Mom and I are okay with that."

Curt usually knew what to say, but not now. How did one respond to a story like hers? The problems he'd faced in life were nothing compared to this. "I'm so sorry,

Taylor. I can't imagine what it's been like for you and your mom."

"Mom struggled with it for a long time. She's doing better, though. I think having Reese helps. It's hard to be upset with her around. And it sounds crazy, but I'm glad Dad wasn't alive when it happened. I think it would've been even harder for him than it was Mom."

He thought of the friendly little girl who wanted to teach him soccer. Curt hadn't known her long, but he agreed with Taylor's comment. "It must've been hard for you, too, when it happened. In essence losing a sister and becoming a parent overnight."

"Yes and no. I'd really hoped she'd get her life together, but part of me knew it wouldn't happen. Some people can't change no matter how much help and support they have. When we found out Eliza had been arrested, it wasn't a surprise. She'd been arrested once before, just not for something serious enough to send her to prison."

Curt agreed. He'd seen a few acquaintances spiral out of control with drugs and alcohol, despite good support systems. As far as he knew none had ended up in prison, but having powerful, influential relatives tended to help with matters such as those. "Is Eliza still in prison?"

Taylor shook her head. "She's out now, but I'm not sure where she is. She called my mom about seven or eight months ago. Said she needed money for food. Mom's heard that too many times to just hand over cash. Mom told Eliza she'd meet her at the store and they'd go shopping together."

He knew the answer to his next question before he asked it. "What happened?"

"She told Mom to forget it and hasn't called since."

Yeah, the answer he'd expected.

"Eliza didn't even ask about Reese the day she called." The bitterness was back in Taylor's voice.

One word described a woman like Eliza Walker: bitch.

"Reese doesn't know any of this. We're waiting until

she's older to tell her everything. For now she just knows her mom couldn't take care of her so she came to live with me. I'm dreading the conversation, but she deserves to know the truth. Mom and I both hope when she learns about Eliza, it'll keep her away from drugs."

"Sounds like the right decision."

Taylor pulled her hand from his and reached for her dessert again. "Enough with this depressing subject. Time for something more interesting."

"Name it."

Genuine curiosity replaced the pain and anger in her eyes. "You."

He'd opened himself up to this by asking about her sister. "Me?"

She'd shared more with him than any other man in recent memory, partly because he'd asked but also because she wanted to. Although there remained a lot she didn't know about Curt, she couldn't ignore the feelings he kicked up inside her. Feelings, both emotional and physical, she wanted to explore. Considering the way he kept looking at her, he wanted to do some exploring, too. At the moment, she wasn't sure if he wanted to explore more than just her body. But since he showed a true interest in her family, she hoped it ran deeper than some simple physical gratification.

"Yeah, you. You said you come from a big family, but don't talk much about them. Do they live around here?" Taylor understood not everyone wanted to share information quite as personal as the details she'd just shared with someone they barely knew. That didn't mean he couldn't offer a little more about his background.

Curt signaled for their server to come over. When she arrived, he requested another espresso. "Do you want anything else, Taylor?" he asked her.

"Sure, why not? Another latte would be fabulous."

After the server left, several seconds passed before he

spoke. "My parents live in Rhode Island. My sister Leah lives in Connecticut. Brett, my older brother, lives wherever Uncle Sam tells him to."

Now they were getting somewhere. He'd shared some actual names with her. She'd noticed up until now he never referred to any family members by name.

"Perhaps about half my family is in the New England area, but I have a few cousins in New York and Virginia. I have at least one cousin out in California. Another was talking about moving there, but I'm not sure if he ever did. We've never been close, so we don't stay in touch. And I have an uncle and aunt in the Washington, D.C. area."

"Sounds like you always have someplace to go on vacation."

"You could say that."

A different server appeared again with their drinks. Taylor didn't miss the once-over the woman gave Curt as she set down his espresso. She couldn't blame the waitress. Curt was too yummy for his own good. There was something else about him, too. This aura of class and power clung to him. Called attention to him. Whatever existed in his background, it didn't include ex-convicts like hers did. Curt didn't seem to mind, though, so she wouldn't worry about it either.

"I love visiting D.C., especially in the springtime before it gets too hot. I was in Virginia for some training last year and spent a day in D.C. before coming home. When Reese gets a little older, Mom and I plan to take her there. A few agents I graduated the academy with work in D.C. but live in Virginia and drive in every day. Does your uncle live in the city or on the outskirts?"

Curt shifted in his seat and reached for his espresso. "My uncle and aunt live right in D.C. They've lived there for several years, but visit New England when they can. They have a beach house in Newport, Rhode Island. And the whole family tries to get together for New Year's Eve. My uncle throws a party every year. There's always at least one person who can't make it. Usually it's my brother."

If Brett lived wherever Uncle Sam told him to, it meant he was in the military. "You don't see your brother much?"

"No. I haven't seen Brett since my cousin's engagement party last summer. I was surprised he even made that. He didn't make Derek's wedding. But we keep in touch."

By the time they left Pellegrino and drove back to their neighborhood, she'd learned a little more about his family. She also learned he'd never had a pet, even though he'd wanted one growing up, because his mother was allergic to animals, and that he loved fresh fruit but detested bananas. Yet even with everything he'd told her, she couldn't shake the feeling there was something he was holding back. Some important detail he didn't feel comfortable enough sharing yet. In time she hoped he would. She could respect and understand someone holding back information for a short time, but she couldn't be with someone who kept secrets. Regardless of anything else, a relationship needed honesty.

"Can I expect you by tomorrow with the pie for comparison purposes?" Curt asked. He'd stopped in her driveway and turned off the engine, but so far made no move to get out. His fingers brushed across her cheek before slipping down her neck. "Or I can bring it to you."

Right now she didn't care about comparing desserts. She was much more interested in tasting him. She planned on doing it, too, before anything else. Leaning across the console separating them, she gently covered his lips with hers. Curt responded immediately, his kiss more a caress that fed the desire building inside her. Each pass of his lips over hers communicated both tenderness and mastery. Needing more, she sucked on his bottom lip until Curt parted his lips. Her tongue tangled with his as his hand explored the bare skin on her back and shoulders. Each movement he made with his mouth and hands sent pleasure radiating from her core to the rest of her body. The console between them made it impossible to press her body against his, to feel his chest against her breasts and his arms around her waist. She considered and quickly dismissed climbing into his lap. She was a little old for straddling a guy in the front seat while they made out. Maybe eighteen years ago she could've justified it, but not now. Besides, Curt might be too refined for such behavior.

They pulled apart at the same time. Curt's hand continued moving across her bare skin as his lips nipped at the skin along her neck.

She slipped her fingers into the hair. It was incredibly soft. "I've got a better idea," she said.

"I'm listening." His warm breath skated across her skin when he answered, and he sounded as breathless as she felt.

"We go back to your house, and I'll let you know about tomorrow later."

***

The windows remained bare, and moonlight spilled into Curt's bedroom. Resting on her side, Taylor used the opportunity the light provided her and allowed her eyes to wander across his chest and down his stomach. Unfortunately, the cotton sheet resting just below his waist prevented her eyes from seeing more. She'd suspected the first day she met him that Curt took care of himself. No one had biceps like his naturally. What she saw now, and had felt earlier when she'd run her hands down his naked back and ass, confirmed her suspicions.

Curt's fingertips brushed against her upper arm, sending her eyes back to his face. At some point after entering his room he'd removed his glasses, and she found herself even more captivated by his eyes than she'd been before. They simply were the most gorgeous shade of blue she'd ever seen.

"Stay the night," he said.

Since becoming Reese's guardian, she'd spent every

night within shouting distance of her niece, except for those times she'd been forced to travel or Reese slept at Hazel's. Sure, Mom was around in case Reese had a bad dream or an emergency arose, but Taylor saw Reese as her responsibility, not Mom's. Responsibility like that meant she came home every night.

"I can't. Not with Reese home. Sorry." Taylor waited for his response. She'd had a similar discussion with a guy she'd dated when Reese had been much younger. He hadn't understood. Instead, he'd insisted Reese would never know the difference and that she'd be okay with her grandmother.

Shifting his position in bed, his fingers moved over her shoulder and toward the sheet covering her breasts. "Do you want me to bring you home now?" Curt kissed the skin exposed above the material and her nipple pebbled against the sheet. He repeated the action on the other side before dipping his tongue into the valley between her breasts. "Or can you stay longer?"

Leave now? Was he crazy? She had a naked man who knew how to pleasure a woman next to her, who was ready to go again. She'd enjoyed herself with men before, but never anywhere near what she'd experienced with Curt. Either the guy had way more experience than she did, or he'd been born with one hell of a special talent.

When he changed his position the sheet dropped lower, but not as much as she would've liked. Tugging the material down, she didn't stop until it reached his midthigh. She traced the well-pronounced vein in his penis before wrapping her hand around him. "How's this for an answer?"

Curt responded with his lips and tongue instead of words.

CHAPTER SEVEN

"So who's the new man in your life?" Mary Jasper, another DEA agent, asked. Mary and Taylor had started with the agency around the same time and shared a cubicle. They were also friends.

Taylor looked up from the document she was reading. "What?"

"Man in your life. Who is he?" Mary asked again, slowly drawing out each word. "Don't bother saying there isn't one. You've got that glow about you."

"Glow? What the heck are talking about?" She'd seen herself in the mirror this morning, and she looked the same as she did every morning.

"Really? I have to spell it out?" Mary rolled her chair across the cubicle. "Everyone gets this look when they start a new relationship. Especially when the sex is good. It wears off over time. You've had it for over a week, my friend. So, who is he? Anyone I know?"

If anyone would know about a look, it would be Mary. The woman dated more than anyone Taylor knew. She'd lost count of how many men Mary had gone out with just in the past twelve months.

"My new neighbor."

"Do tell." Mary leaned on Taylor's desk, apparently not moving until she got some information.

She gave Mary enough information to hopefully satisfy her curiosity without sharing intimate details.

"Has he met Reese and your mom?" Mary asked.

Mary knew all about Dennis, and why Taylor had put an end to their relationship. "Oh, yeah. He's come over for dinner a few times, and Reese is teaching him to play soccer. She gave him his second lesson Tuesday night."

Unfortunately, she'd missed seeing both lessons because of work, but Mom filled her in on them. Mom said if she didn't know better she'd think Curt had children of his own, considering how he interacted with Reese.

"Wow. Now, that's impressive. Especially since you were here with me until nine o'clock Tuesday night. Sounds like this guy might have real potential."

What would Mary think if she told her what he'd done last night? Taylor and Reese had been clearing off the table after dinner when Curt rang the doorbell, a well-used lacrosse stick in one hand and a pink one still in its packaging in the other. He'd then spent the next hour in the backyard, giving Reese a lesson.

"He might." Everything pointed toward Mary being correct. However, it took more than a couple weeks and a few meals to really know someone.

"Maybe the two of you can come out with Aaron and me some night."

"Aaron? I thought you were dating someone named Randy."

Mary waved her hand. "Stopped seeing Randy two months ago. The jerk was married. Well, actually, separated… so that's a little better. But he never bothered to tell me. We saw his wife while having dinner. She was out with some friends. Talk about a little awkward."

The woman really did go through men quickly.

"Aaron and I have been together since last month. He's a special agent with the FBI. We worked on a case together back in January and bumped into each other outside Faneuil Hall one afternoon. He asked me to dinner, and we've been together since."

Taylor ran through the agents she knew in the Boston FBI office. She only knew of one Aaron. "Are you talking about Aaron Linz?" She'd done an arrest with the agent, and he'd come across as a nice man.

Mary nodded, but Taylor's ringing cell phone prevented her from adding any more details. And Mary liked sharing details, no matter how personal and intimate. It was the biggest difference between them.

The name Curt on the screen sent a bolt of excitement through her. She didn't hesitate to answer. "Hey, you." He'd called her a few times, but never in the middle of a workday.

"Hey, yourself." Curt's voice washed over her, and suddenly the cubicle became too warm.

Taylor considered using the file folder as a fan, but decided against it with Mary sitting next to her. "Is everything okay?" He wouldn't call to simply chat in the middle of the afternoon. There had to be a reason. Had something happened at home and Mom was unable to call?

"Fine. But it'd be even better if you were with me."

The guy was good. No question about it.

"I'm on Newbury Street right now. Are you available for lunch or coffee?" Curt asked.

She'd planned to eat the lunch she'd packed at her desk, like she did most days. She found it saved money, because eating out every day in downtown Boston quickly added up, no matter how frugal you were with your choices.

"Sure. Just tell me when and where and I'll meet you."

Next to her Mary checked her e-mails, but it was obvious she listened in on Taylor's half of the conversation.

"How about we meet in twenty minutes at Faneuil

Hall, near the statue of Samuel Adams."

Twenty minutes gave her enough time to answer whatever questions Mary had rolling around in her head and walk over to the marketplace. "Sounds good. See you then."

The questions started as soon as she put the cell phone down.

***

Located behind Faneuil Hall on Congress Street, the large bronze statue of Samuel Adams, one of America's founding fathers, was a favorite photo spot for visitors to Boston. Today was no different. Despite the crowd around the area, she spotted Curt right away. Although dressed like many of the people around him, he stood out in the crowd. Something other than his looks drew your attention his way. She'd noticed it before, but still couldn't put her finger on what it was about him.

Taylor let her gaze linger. The jeans and navy-blue polo shirt did nothing to hide the body she knew they covered. The glances other women in the vicinity sent his way as they passed told her she wasn't the only one to think so. The dark sunglasses made it impossible to see Curt's eyes, but she got the impression he paid no attention to the women passing by him. Even when a woman with a body and face worthy of a magazine cover walked by and smiled, he remained expressionless.

Until he spotted her.

His smile encompassed his entire face, and again she wished she could fan herself.

Good thing he's not smiling at any of the women around him, she thought. If he did, they'd never leave him alone. He'd almost reached her when she realized she hadn't taken a step since she first stopped. *Get moving.*

"Great timing." He greeted her with a hug and kiss, earning her some looks of envy from the females nearby. "How much time do you have?"

Unlike her first part-time job while in high school, she

didn't get a set amount of time for a lunch break. "I can't take all day, but I don't need to rush back either."

"How does a picnic sound? We can grab something here and take it over to the Common."

"I like your plan."

Faneuil Hall Marketplace offered every type of food imaginable. Sometimes Taylor thought it had too much to pick from because, when she did come over, she found it hard to decide. Rather than waste time today and linger over the various menus, she followed Curt's lead and ordered a roasted vegetable flatbread and a piece of Greek baklava at the Mediterranean deli. As she expected, he refused to let her pay for her lunch. Instead, he promised she could get it next time. With so many people around them she didn't argue, but later she planned on saying something. This was the second time he'd given her the same line.

The oldest park in the United States, the Boston Common attracted Boston residents as well as out of town visitors. The fifty-acre park was an oasis of open space, green grass, and trees nestled in the bustling city. Today, people from all backgrounds occupied the Common and enjoyed the beautiful spring day.

They walked until Curt found them a fairly secluded bench in the shade. Away from any large groups and onlookers, he put the bag containing their lunch on the bench and wrapped his arms around her. His mouth came down hard on hers while his fingers spread across her back. Heat seeped through her blouse and warmed her skin.

"I dreamed about you last night." He moved his lips away from her mouth and near her ear. Curt's fingers moved up her spine, each touch setting off a thousand fireworks in her body.

"A good dream, I hope."

"Good, but it would've been better if it'd been real." His fingers hit the edge of her bra and started the trip back down toward her waist.

"And what were we doing?"

Curt brushed a kiss against the pulse in her neck, the tiny action causing it to accelerate. "What do you think?" When he reached her waist, he didn't stop. Instead, his hands slid over her ass as he kissed her neck again.

Taylor pulled herself out of the sensual haze clouding her head. It was either that or suggest they find a hotel room for an hour or so. "Playing soccer in my backyard? That's what we were doing in the dream I had about you." Laughter was a good remedy for many aliments, including sexual arousal when you couldn't do anything about it.

The comment earned her a light swat on ass. "Not even close," he grumbled. "Should I tell you?"

Reaching for his sunglasses, she pushed them up onto his head so she could see his eyes. "Maybe you can show me later. I suspect it'll be much more fun than hearing about it."

"You're right." He let her go so they could both sit down. Then he started unpacking their lunch. He started to hand over her sandwich, but stopped. "Did you really dream we were playing soccer?"

Taylor took the sandwich from his hand. "Don't worry, we were alone… and you were naked." She wiggled her eyebrows and smiled.

"It'd be more fun if we both were naked."

She agreed but kept silent. A few hours of the workday remained, so this was not the time to be hot and bothered.

Curt plucked the sunglasses off his head and slipped them back into place. Having them on protected his eyes and identity. She'd seen him a few times without glasses. During those times, she'd never shown any indication she recognized him as Curt Sherbrooke. However, all those times had occurred in his bed. If she was concentrating only on his eyes and face when they made love, he was doing something very wrong.

"Not that I'm not glad to see you, but what are doing in Boston today?" Taylor pulled her hair back in a loose ponytail before she unwrapped her flatbread.

"I stopped at King Lighting in Watertown. Since I was in the general area I went over to Newbury Street, looking for a Mother's Day present."

He'd already visited several stores in New Hampshire but hadn't found any light fixtures for the kitchen. In the past he'd had success at King Lighting, so he made the trip south, and took advantage of the opportunity to shop, and stop at his place in Boston to pick up some items he wanted. He left the final stop of his day off his itinerary. Telling Taylor he kept a condo in Boston would bring up other questions. Answers to those questions might leave Taylor wondering things about him he didn't want her wondering today.

"Any luck?" Taylor asked, taking a bite of her lunch and swallowing.

"Yes, on both counts."

"I have no idea what to get Mom this year. She's never been the easiest person to shop for." She raised her sandwich toward her mouth, but stopped short of biting into it again.

If Taylor thought Priscilla was hard, she should meet his mother. When the woman wanted something, she went out and bought it. And forget about there being anything she needed. That scenario did not exist. Ever.

"Last year I got her a gift certificate for a day at a spa. One of those special packages that includes a facial, manicure, and a pedicure. She almost never pampers herself. She loved it, but I don't want to do the same thing again."

He didn't have Mom's weekly schedule, but he was confident she got all three of those things on a regular basis.

"What did you get? Maybe it'll give me a new idea."

Please don't ask to see it. One look at it would send

Taylor's mind in a direction he didn't need it going. "Jewelry." His mother had no need for more, but when he saw the one-of-a-kind diamond-and-emerald necklace, he'd known his mom would love it. Emeralds were her favorite gemstone.

Taylor played with the sandwich wrapper. "Yeah, that's out. I got Mom a bracelet for her birthday in February. And for Christmas I got her a new purse, so that's not an option either." She sighed as she wrapped the untouched half of her sandwich and put it back inside the plastic bag. Then she went for the baklava she'd ordered. "Maybe I'll take Reese shopping this weekend after her soccer game. It'll be just the two of us. Mom can't come—she's got plans with a friend. She loves gardening; we might find something at the Green Caterpillar. It's a gardening store in Nashua. And Nashua isn't very far away."

"Other than Reese's soccer game, do you have any plans this weekend?"

Her head tipped back, and she looked at the sky. "I told Mom I'd cut the lawn. We usually take turns doing it, but her knee has been bothering her again. If I don't do it soon, Stripes will get lost every time he goes out."

He'd offer to do it, but he'd never touched a lawn mower in his life.

"Reese's game isn't until noon on Saturday and it's in town, so I'm hoping to get the lawn done in the morning before we go."

"Want some company at the game?"

"*You* want to come and watch a bunch of seven-year-olds play soccer?"

Right now he wasn't sure who was more surprised by his question: her or him. He'd asked about her weekend plans because he wanted to get her alone again, not because he had a dying need to see a children's soccer game. But he knew a mother/daughter bond existed between Taylor and her niece. He'd never ask Taylor to skip events with Reese to be with him instead.

Curt shrugged. "Why not?" *Because you're getting yourself in deeper and deeper each time you interact with Taylor and her family.* And the deeper he got, the shittier he felt, because they didn't know who he really was. "Maybe I'll learn a thing or two watching them."

"Okay, but don't complain or ask me to rub it when your butt hurts from sitting on the metal bleachers all afternoon."

"What if I return the favor? I'm very good at giving massages." Curt set aside his sandwich, and angled her body so he could rub her shoulders. While his fingers kneaded the knots there, he kissed the side of her neck. "Come by tonight and I'll give you a more thorough demonstration." He moved his hands lower and massaged the area between her shoulder blades. "Of course, you could repay the favor if you were so inclined."

She groaned when he started working out a large knot. "I can't tonight. Can I get a rain check?"

Her request brought to mind another conversation. "Did Reese ever learn why we call it a rain check?"

"Huh?" She glanced over her shoulder.

Curt continued the massage while he explained his conversation with Reese.

"She never asked me about it. Maybe Mom found her an answer."

The girl seemed like the type who'd seek out an answer whenever something she didn't understand or know crossed her path. "I'll ask her." He kissed her neck again. "You can collect your rain check whenever you want," he said.

***

A little more than an hour later, Curt escorted Taylor back and made a hasty retreat from the city. Rush hour traffic out of Boston didn't start at five like many people thought. No, around here the highways became a parking lot starting at three thirty, and he had no desire to be stuck sitting there.

Because he intended to pick stuff up from his condo, he'd left his motorcycle in the garage and driven his SUV into the city this morning. The weather, though, called for either the bike or the new Aston Martin convertible sitting in Newport. He'd only driven the car twice since purchasing it. He needed to rectify that soon. While the SUV got him where he needed to go, it lacked style and personality. *But it blends in well,* he reminded himself. Every other household in Pelham either owned a SUV, minivan, or a pickup. He'd seen plenty of BMWs and Mercedes in town, as well as a few Porsches. Still, if he showed up at the grocery store on Route 38 in either his Aston Martin or the McLaren, people would notice. Once they noticed, somehow word would get back to Taylor and her family. Information such as that needed to come from him, not some third party. Assuming she needed the information at all. At the moment, he wasn't sure she did.

"Keep offering to attend her niece's soccer games and you'll need to share." He never should've opened his damn mouth. He would've survived until Sunday without any female companionship. Getting involved with a woman hadn't even been part of his plan when he moved.

"You came here to finish the book and renovate a house." A house he planned on selling when complete, so he could move on to another project. One located in New England, or just about anywhere else in the country. Oddly, the longer he lived in the house and the town, the less appealing the thought of selling it became.

CHAPTER EIGHT

She filled two quart-sized containers with fresh strawberries. The day before, she and Reese had gone strawberry picking at Nash Farm, a family-owned farm in town. They usually went three or four times a year. It was a tradition she'd started right after Reese started walking. Since then they'd added blueberry and raspberry picking in the summer and, of course, apple picking in the fall. Often, they'd eat some of what they picked then Mom would use some to make strawberry jam before freezing the rest. Rather than freeze any this time, Mom suggested she bring some with her when she went over to Curt's house. She'd last seen him Friday night after work. Reese had insisted she should ask him to come strawberry picking with them, but she hadn't mentioned it. As much as she enjoyed spending time with him, there were some traditions she didn't want anyone, including Curt, intruding on. Yesterday's outing was one of them. Turned out he had plans anyway. He hadn't gone into detail, but let her know he was attending his cousin's bachelor party in Rhode Island.

"Good, you remembered the strawberries." Mom walked into the kitchen, Reese trailing behind her. They both had on old clothes and hats. She stole a strawberry from the large bowl Taylor hadn't yet put away. "Reese and I are going to start on the garden. Hopefully, by the time you come home, we'll have most of the plants in the ground."

Growing up, Taylor had helped Mom plant seeds in the fenced garden area behind the house. After too many years of plants not growing well, Mom had switched her strategy. Now she planted the seeds in special containers in the house. Once they were large enough, she transplanted them into the ground. She'd noticed yesterday that Mom had carried all the containers outside to the patio.

"Have fun. What are you planting this year?"

Although she never enjoyed helping, she did like having the fresh vegetables in the house. The tomatoes and carrots from the store didn't come close to tasting as good as the ones from Mom's garden. Reese seemed to like helping with the garden. She even did some of the weeding and watering as the growing season progressed.

"Tomatoes, carrots, cucumbers, peppers." Reese counted each one off on her fingers as she went along. Taylor noticed she'd already slipped on her new gardening gloves, the ones the Easter bunny had left in her basket this year, along with a new bathing suit. "Did I miss anything, Mimi?"

"And zucchini. Hopefully, it does better this year." Mom added the last item to Reese's list.

"Sounds like we'll have a lot of fresh veggies this summer."

"Where are you and Curt going on your date, Auntie?"

She had no idea. He'd asked her to leave today open, but hadn't shared any other details. So far, she'd enjoyed the time she'd spent with him. She expected the same to be true today. "I don't know."

"Tell him you want to go to Jump." Reese loved the new indoor trampoline park that had opened over the winter in Manchester.

Taylor gathered up the containers and her keys. "I don't think he'll want to go there today." She didn't want to go there either. She'd seen adults enjoying Jump. The place even had a ladies' night once a week for everyone over twenty-one, and a competitive dodge ball league for anyone over eighteen. But while she took Reese and her friends there all the time because they loved it, she had no interest in going without them. Curt didn't seem like the type to enjoy the place either.

The motorcycle parked near the front door with two helmets dangling from the handlebars gave her a small clue of their plans today. He'd mentioned owning one, but she'd never seen him use it.

She paused and looked over the bike. She'd passed them countless times in parking lots but never got too close. Today she did, because Curt wouldn't mind if she took a closer look. The instrument panel appeared to contain gauges similar to those in a car. She didn't recognize the company emblem on the motorcycle, but it appeared to be a top-of-the line model. This didn't look like the type of bike a man would put in front of his house with a For Sale sign attached. They'd never discussed finances, but if his book had been as big a hit as Mom claimed *and* he'd left his full-time job in Boston, she assumed he was doing rather well for himself. Not to mention all the money he must be putting into the renovation of the house. Even smaller jobs, like when Dad redid the kitchen floor, became costly. Redoing an entire house had to be insanely expensive, even if Curt was doing most of the work himself.

"Just on my way to get you. I thought you'd forgotten about me." Curt walked down the front steps and across the walkway.

Like any woman could forget him, and he knew it. Not that he was conceited about it, but he had a confidence about him that let Taylor know he knew the kind of effect he had on the opposite sex.

"Well, I wanted to help them plant the garden, but Reese reminded me you and I have plans today." She enjoyed teasing him, and he often reciprocated.

Slipping his arms around her, he smiled. "I'll have to thank her later. Right now, I want to concentrate on you." His voice became low and sensual. "I missed you last night."

Curt's hands traveled lower, slipping into her back pockets, and he traced her lips for a moment before kissing her. He kept the kiss slow and undemanding, but still shivers of desire raced through her. When he did pull away, she contemplated pulling his face back to hers and enjoying herself more. The strawberries she held made it impossible.

"I missed you, too. Did you have fun at the party?"

"Are you asking if I had fun, or do you really want to know if I behaved myself?" Curt asked.

She worked with enough men to know what sometimes went on at bachelor parties. Curt seemed too classy to partake in those kinds of things, but when guys got together, stuff happened. "Maybe both," she reluctantly admitted.

"Yes, I had fun, and yes, I behaved myself. We went to a rock climbing gym not far from Providence. My uncle Mark and father came, too. Afterwards, we went for drinks at a club downtown. As far as bachelor parties go, it was enjoyable but tame. The kind I prefer."

She'd never met his relatives, but she liked them already. "I'm glad you had fun."

"What did you do yesterday?"

"After strawberry picking, we had a family game night." It killed her to do so, but she pulled away from him and held up the containers she carried. "I brought you some of them."

"Isn't it a little early for strawberry picking around here?" Curt asked, accepting the containers.

"For strawberries planted outside, yes. These were

grown in the farm's giant, or as Reese calls it, ginormous greenhouse. Sometime in June we'll go again and pick the ones growing outside."

"Never heard of a farm growing strawberries indoors."

"I think Nash Farm in town might be the only one. At least the only one in this area, and the greenhouse isn't open to the public. A friend from high school married into the family that owns the farm. Her daughter and Reese are in the same grade and get along really well. A few years ago the family had a mammoth greenhouse built on the property, and they grow various fruits and vegetables inside it year round. They let us come and pick strawberries before the season starts. Later in June and July, we'll go back and pick outside with the rest of the paying customers."

"Sounds like a good deal." Curt opened a container and sampled one. Red strawberry juice clung to his lips, tempting her to lick it off. "Wow, these are good. Much better than the ones from the store." He plucked out two more before covering the bowl again. "We'll have them when we come back."

"Speaking of coming back, where are we going?"

"It's supposed to be beautiful all day. I thought we'd take a ride up north along the Kancamagus Highway. Maybe do some hiking or check out Echo Lake or the Flume Gorge. My cousin told me about a place called Polly's Pancake Parlor. It's not far from the highway and serves breakfast all day. Says he stops there all the time when he's in the area, because they have the best pancakes he's ever tasted."

"He's right. Whenever we go up that way we stop at Polly's. Reese swears even their chocolate milk is better than what we make at home. It tastes the same to me. What does your cousin do that sends him up there?"

Curt looked down at the containers he held, making it difficult to see his eyes. "He works for a big hotel chain. He's the regional director for the Northeast." He still didn't look at her as he reopened the container and took out two more strawberries. "These really are delicious. Thanks for sharing."

"And he's the cousin getting married." Could anyone blame her for wanting to learn more about his family? Not only did he know a great deal about hers, but he frequently joined them for dinner.

"No. Trent's married. It's his younger brother who's getting married in June," Curt answered. "Let me put these away and we'll go." He covered the plastic bowls and turned.

She watched him walk away, admiring the way his powerful, well-muscled body moved. When the door closed behind him, her attention transferred to their conversation. At least now she had another name to associate with Curt's family. He hadn't given up very many since the night at Pellegrino.

***

Curt came out of the curve in the road and accelerated. The Kancamagus Highway had been made for motorcycle rides. The thirty-four-and-a-half-mile road stretched from Lincoln, New Hampshire, to Conway, and cut through the White Mountains National Forest. Nature surrounded them on both sides, the occasional parking area or entrance to a camping ground the only thing to break up the natural beauty. This was the second time he'd driven along the road, but once again the views took his breath away. He read they were even better in the fall when foliage turned the landscape into a masterpiece of color. This September or October he'd make sure to come back through the area.

Taylor leaned into his back, and her arms tightened around his waist. He'd never taken anyone out for a ride. None of the women he'd dated before had mentioned it, and he'd never asked them. When Taylor commented she'd never been on a motorcycle but would love to try, he'd known he had to be the one to take her. The mere thought of her intimately pressed up against another man like she was against him now had left him gritting his teeth. Definitely not a rational response, but he'd been unable to shake it.

After today, every time he got on the bike he'd remember what it felt like having her behind him, her breasts pressed against his back and her arms around him.

Another checkmark in the "not good" category. The number of checkmarks there was mounting up.

Both Trent and Gray had questioned him last night about the status of his and Taylor's relationship. When he'd admitted things had progressed past one simple dinner, they'd both offered up their wisdom again. He automatically told them both where they could shove it. That didn't change the fact that they were right.

Turned out, keeping his real identity a secret by telling his neighbors half-truths was much harder to do than he'd expected. Especially when you were sleeping with one of those neighbors.

The conversation they had before leaving reminded him how easily he could slip up. Whenever possible, he avoided mentioning his family. Yet today he'd spoken without thinking when she asked about their plans. After he mentioned his cousin made frequent trips to the northern part of the state, she asked more about him. It was a logical progression for the conversation. After all, it wasn't an area of the state one normally associated with business travel. There were no large cities up this way, or manufacturing centers. Instead, the area was known for skiing in the winter and hiking and camping in the summer.

He'd answered her questions with enough information to satisfy her curiosity but not associate him with the Sherbrooke family. *I hope.* Curt could no longer deny he had to tell Taylor and her mother the truth. He just wasn't ready or willing to do it yet.

***

"Have you been here before?" Curt climbed off the motorcycle and hung his helmet from the handlebars. Then he took hers and did the same. They were parked outside the visitor's center to the Flume Gorge.

"A few times as a kid with my parents and once with Reese last summer."

Curt held her hand as they walked toward the center's entrance built at the base of Mount Liberty. "What should I expect? The website I checked out only said this was a must-see up here."

"A lot of uphill walking and stairs. There's a nice waterfall and what they call the Pool. It's a deep basin in the Pemigewasset River. And if you're brave enough, we can go through the Wolf Den."

"Don't think I like the idea of going through anything with the word 'wolf' attached to it."

Taylor laughed, causing other visitors to glance their way. "Chicken." She gave him a gentle elbow in the side. "It doesn't contain any wolves. It's a narrow one-way path through rocks. It reminds me a little of the Lemon Squeeze at the Polar Caves."

Curt paid the admission to the state park and accepted the guide map the gentleman manning the desk handed him. "I've never heard of the Polar Caves. Care to enlighten me?"

Taylor looked at him as if he'd just said he came from Mars. "Let me make sure I've got this right. You grew up in New England, but never went to the Polar Caves? Next you're going to tell me you never took a family vacation to Santa's Village or Story Land either."

He should've kept his mouth shut and acted like he knew what she was talking about. Too late now, the damage was done.

"I never visited either of those places." He couldn't recall even hearing about them. "They're located around here, too?"

"Uh, yeah. I assumed every kid within driving distance

visited at least one of them before they got too old. They're both amusement parks designed specifically for kids. No giant roller coasters or super crazy rides like most parks. Story Land has characters like Humpty Dumpty, the Old Women in the Shoe, and Cinderella. You can ride around in a giant pumpkin-shaped coach. Santa's Village is always decorated for Christmas. You can visit Santa in his house and have your picture taken with him. You can also feed his reindeer. They're both nice family places. Reese loves to go. I did when I was younger. Mom and Dad took us every summer until I was about eleven. Then the rides were too tame, so we went to bigger amusement parks like Six Flags."

While Taylor told him about the places he'd never visited, they started their trek through the gorge.

"If you didn't ever come up here on vacation, where did you and your family go?"

Another loaded question. He couldn't tell her he'd traveled around the world for family vacations. Most people didn't take those types of trips with kids. Many didn't take them, period. He couldn't tell her he never went anywhere either. She'd never buy it.

"Whatever Mom found interesting that year. She always planned our vacations. We also spent time at my uncle's beach house in Newport." Calling Cliff House, the Sherbrooke family estate on Bellevue Avenue, a beach house was a stretch. Yet not technically wrong, and he had visited there regularly throughout his childhood.

Taylor accepted his answer without question. "Reese wants to go to Santa's Village again this summer. She likes it better than Story Land. I think I do, too. We haven't decided if that's what we're going to do or not. Mom wants to rent a house at the beach for a week instead."

A group of young twentysomething-year-olds passed them, and Curt held off asking any more questions until they were again alone on the path. "And you?"

"Not really sure. A week at the beach might be nice.

Something different. I've taken Reese to the beaches in Hampton and in Rye, but always just for the day. She loves swimming, but I think she'd like the amusement park more than a whole week at the beach."

He came close to suggesting doing both. He caught himself before he put his foot in his mouth again. He doubted Taylor got much more than a few weeks' paid vacation. Even if she got enough for two such vacations, there was the cost to consider.

"You'll figure it out." Before he said anything else that required he either give away too much information or lie, he changed the subject.

CHAPTER NINE

"Auntie Taylor, are you up?"

I am now. Taylor squinted at the ceiling with one eye. Bright sunlight filled the room, a stark contrast to the previous morning. Yesterday, like every day for the past week, it had rained. Last night the town had even sent out an e-mail canceling all soccer games today because the fields resembled muddy swamps. Reese wasn't happy when she found out her game was canceled. Taylor, on the other hand, had been okay with it because it meant she could sleep a little longer today. Or, that had been her plan. Sounded like Reese had other ones for her this morning.

"Yep, come on in." She pried her other eyelid open and waited.

The door opened and the tornado named Reese flew inside, jumped on the bed, and snuggled up next to her. She was already dressed, complete with flip-flops; her hair was pulled up in two pigtails. "Mimi and I are going to the mall to get me new sneakers and some more shorts."

They'd bought Reese new sneakers around Christmas, and she'd already outgrown them. And because she'd grown several inches since last summer, none of her old shorts fit well.

"After, we're going to the grocery store," Reese said.

Better Mom and Reese than her. She avoided both malls and grocery stores and did as much shopping on the Internet as she could.

"We're going to make Boston cream pie to bring to Curt's tonight. Mimi promised we could get some ice cream to bring, too, because I don't like that."

Taylor kissed her niece's head and wrapped an arm around her. "Sounds great. I love Boston cream pie and can't wait to taste it."

She stifled a yawn and wondered how likely it was she'd fall back to sleep after they left. She'd always had sleep issues, and once awake that was usually it for the day. If she had the house to herself for a while, maybe she'd get lucky this morning.

Stripes took the open bedroom door as his invitation to join them. When he jumped onto the bed, Reese sat up and rubbed his head. "Do you want to come shopping with us, Auntie Taylor?"

She'd rather face a whole armed street gang than venture to the mall today or any other day. "I'm not even dressed. You guys go without me. I'll come along next time."

"Come on, Reese. We need to get moving if we're going to have time to bake." Mom entered the bedroom, her keys and purse in hand already.

"See ya." Reese planted a kiss on her cheek before leaping from the bed like a jack-in-the-box. The sudden movement earned her a dirty look from the cat. He'd found the perfect spot in the sun and proceeded to groom himself.

"We'll be back," Mom said. "Do you need anything while we're out?" Mom knew how much she disliked shopping, and if already out she picked up stuff for her.

"All set, I think."

"Call if you change your mind. I left some pancakes in the refrigerator for you."

Taylor yawned again as the bedroom door closed. How long would they be gone? Reese loved the hunt. Usually Mom indulged her and allowed her to try on as many outfits as she wanted. Today she'd have to rein Reese in, though, if they hoped to bake dessert. Mom always insisted on bringing something when invited to someone's house, even if it was only for a cookout like tonight. She'd instilled the belief in Taylor as well, and since Curt had showed up with wine the first night he had dinner with them weeks ago, she guessed he'd been taught the same thing. Right along with opening doors and pulling out chairs for women.

Rolling over, thoughts of falling back to sleep faded. They were replaced by thoughts of their neighbor and the adult activities she'd enjoyed again in his bed last night.

Over the past several weeks, Curt had become a permanent fixture in her life. She refrained from using the word boyfriend when thinking or talking about him. She hadn't attached the label to anyone in years. The word simply hadn't fit any of the men she'd dated since becoming Reese's guardian. Yet, it described the situation between them.

Over the past month and half, they'd gone to the movies and for rides on his motorcycle. She'd helped him put together the new patio furniture he'd bought, and together they'd opened the in-ground pool at his house. She'd taken him to the range for a shooting lesson one night after work, and he'd come to watch one of Reese's soccer games. Twice he'd been in Boston and met her for lunch. Not to mention all the times he'd joined her, Reese, and Mom for dinner. And often after dinner he'd either play soccer with Reese or give her another lacrosse lesson. Much to Reese's annoyance, they hadn't done either all week, first because of special activities at school, and then thanks to the rain. Today promised to be a gorgeous day, and Reese was itching to get Curt outside. No doubt about it, Reese was crazy about the guy.

She'd never admit it out loud, but she had it bad for Curt, too. Any woman would. He was thoughtful and considerate. He actually listened when she spoke to him. Asked her questions about her day and her job. He paid attention to her niece and treated her with respect rather than as an annoyance, no matter how much she talked his ear off. *Don't forget, he's great in bed.*

Vivid memories from the night before flooded her mind, and heat exploded in her stomach.

Their first time together had been incredible, but she'd assumed it had been a fluke, that the sex had been so good because it'd been such a long time since she'd last been with a man. Numerous times later, she knew better. Her long stretch of abstinence had nothing to do with it. Curt was just a damn good lover. He never rushed. He took his time learning her body and what she liked. He never stopped until she lost control and spiraled off the planet for a few blissful moments. No two ways about it, every woman deserved a lover like Curt at least once in her life. And she always did her best to return the favor. Judging by the sounds he made, Taylor figured she succeeded every time.

All those things aside, every once in a while she sensed something was off. More than once she'd caught this almost guilty look in his eyes, as if he had some secret he didn't want to share. Each time, it disappeared almost as quickly as it appeared, making her wonder if she'd imagined it. She spent so much time around criminals who lied and did anything they could to protect their butts that maybe she saw things that weren't there. Mom never mentioned having any suspicions, and she had no problem letting him be around Reese. If Mom sensed Curt was harboring some deep, dark secret, she wouldn't invite him over on a regular basis and let him play soccer with Reese in the backyard. No, she might be a more trusting person than Taylor, but Priscilla Walker would never jeopardize her granddaughter's safety.

Taylor kicked off the blankets and sat up. "No chance of me getting back to sleep." She had the erotic memories of last night to thank for that. Still, it'd be nice to have an empty house for a few hours. She could enjoy a coffee and then a long, hot shower before breakfast, something her schedule didn't regularly allow. During the week, if she hoped to get a jump on traffic into Boston, she had to leave early. Even on the weekends, leisurely showers didn't fit into her life. Today she had the opportunity and planned on taking it.

She found the stack of blueberry pancakes in the refrigerator and popped a few of them into the microwave. While they heated, she prepared another cup of coffee. The sound of a car outside had her pausing before she got the mug to her lips.

She'd taken her time in the shower, but not so long that Mom and Reese could be back already, even if Mom had really reined Reese in. The ringing doorbell verified it wasn't them. With the house set so far back from the road, random strangers rarely rang the bell. Even during the last election, when minions for the various candidates had gone from door to door hoping to drum up support, no one had visited them—unlike many of their various neighbors. She'd heard people in town complain that sometimes three or four different people visited their doorsteps.

Was it Curt? He'd said he planned on spending the morning working on his book, but maybe he'd changed his mind. Or needed a break from his computer screen.

Almost immediately the doorbell rang again, and she dismissed the idea that it was Curt. Whoever was outside lacked patience. In no great rush, Taylor sipped her coffee as she left the kitchen.

"Hey, sis," the visitor greeted when Taylor opened the door.

Taylor choked on her coffee. A coughing fit made it impossible to speak for several seconds. Even after it subsided Taylor stood there and stared, speechless. After working as a police officer, and now a DEA agent, nothing surprised her anymore—or so she'd thought until this very moment. Finding her older sister ringing the bell had done it.

Eliza walked past Taylor and entered the house before Taylor could decide whether to tell her to leave or invite her in. "Aren't you going to say something?" Eliza asked, her voice grating on Taylor's ears.

She'd aged fifteen years since Taylor had last seen her. Her hair, the same shade as Reese's, hung limply to her shoulders and it looked like she hadn't washed it in several days. Deep wrinkles fanned out near her eyes and around her mouth. And her clothes hung off her sickly, thin frame.

Taylor skipped the small talk. If Eliza was here, she wanted something. "What are you doing here?"

Turning, Eliza smiled—revealing her two missing bottom teeth. "I came to wish Mom a happy Mother's Day." She glanced around before walking down the hall toward the kitchen. "Something smells good. Is there any breakfast left? I'm starving."

Since it looked like Eliza hadn't eaten in more than a week, Taylor didn't doubt it. She followed closely behind, prepared to tell her sister to get lost as soon as Eliza shared why she was really there. "Mother's Day already went by."

Eliza went straight for the extra pancakes Taylor hadn't heated in the microwave, and dug in without sitting down. "You know I'm not great with dates." She paused long enough to pour herself a coffee before going back to shoveling food into her mouth as if their mother had never taught them any table manners. "Where are Mom and Reese?"

"Shopping. You could've called and wished Mom a happy Mother's Day. Her number hasn't changed." Their mother had had the same phone number since she'd gotten her very first cell phone a decade ago. And the house number was the same one they'd had growing up.

Whatever Eliza's reason for being here, it had nothing to do with Mom. The woman never visited or even called for her daughter's birthday, so there was no way she'd stop by because she suddenly wanted to wish their mom a happy Mother's Day.

Her sister shrugged. "I was in the area." Eliza finished off her pancakes and looked at Taylor. "Are there any more?"

Her sister looked like she needed them a hell of lot more than she did. "In the microwave. Help yourself."

Eliza went straight for them and dug in with almost as much gusto as she had with the first few. "You look ready to go out. Got big plans today? Don't worry about me. I'll hang around and wait for Mom."

Like she'd ever leave Eliza alone in the house. "Later this afternoon I have plans." She watched her older sister, a woman she didn't know anymore, devour the food she'd heated up for herself. Getting a straight answer was probably too much to ask for. Instead of trying, she'd let Eliza finish eating and then ask her to leave.

"What about Mom and Reese? Will they be back soon, or are they gone for the day?"

Taylor had a sneaking suspicion she knew why Eliza was interested in their plans. It was much easier to steal from a house when you knew it was empty. Taylor knew Eliza would stoop low enough to steal from her own family. She'd done it before. Or at least, Taylor was confident she had. Before Eliza's stint in rehab, someone had broken into the house. Several pieces of Mom's jewelry had disappeared, but oddly none of her favorites—including the diamond anniversary band Dad gave her for their twentieth anniversary. Some of Dad's expensive power tools had also been taken, as well as an antique table clock. The thief left behind Mom's laptop and her top-of-the-line camera, even though they'd both been out in plain sight. And the intruder had been amazingly neat and tidy, too. They hadn't dumped drawers on the floor searching for items or broken a single thing. In her experience intruders didn't care if they made a mess, and they didn't leave behind diamond rings or expensive cameras. Not unless they knew how much they meant to their owners.

"They'll be back very soon. Reese has a friend coming over for the night." If it meant Eliza wouldn't try sneaking back in later, she'd lie. "And you can*not* be here when they get home."

Eliza might be Reese's mother, but Taylor wasn't comfortable with her niece meeting her. She didn't believe her sister would ever physically hurt Reese, but such a meeting might cause emotional damage. Right now, Reese seemed like a well-adjusted young girl. It didn't make sense to jeopardize that.

"Last time I checked, Mom owned this house, not you. She gets to decide who visits, and she never told me I wasn't welcome, Sis."

A sharp pain went through her jaw, and Taylor relaxed her mouth. Short of murdering someone, Taylor couldn't think of a single thing her sister could do that would cause Mom to bar Eliza from the house. Mom might hate the decisions Eliza had made in life, but she still loved her oldest daughter.

"Do you really think being here when Reese comes home is a good idea?" Highly unlikely, but maybe her sister would use some common sense for her daughter's sake.

Eliza shrugged, and Taylor knew she wouldn't like her answer. "Don't see the big deal. She's *my* daughter."

She saw red when she heard the emphasis Eliza put on "my." The woman might have carried Reese for nine months, but Taylor was more Reese's mom than Eliza was. Not once since she'd given up custody had Eliza sent a letter or a card to the little girl. She never called and inquired about her well-being. Instead, she acted like she never had a child. In Taylor's book that was A-OK. Reese was much better off without Eliza in her life. "Just because you gave birth to her doesn't mean anything, and you damn well know it."

"Kind of hard to be a mom when you're in jail."

Nope, she wouldn't let Eliza use that as an excuse. "And whose fault is that, Eliza? Not mine or Mom's. They have paper and pens in prison. They let you send letters. You could have kept in contact. And you've been out for how long now? A couple years? Yet you never call and ask about her? Even on her birthdays you don't call."

"How do you stand always being Little Miss Perfect? Don't you ever get tired of it?"

Eliza had called her the same thing when they were kids. Today it annoyed her just as much as it had back then.

The sound of the front door opening made Taylor's stomach roll.

"Auntie Taylor, we're home!" Reese's voice entered the kitchen before she did.

Both Mom and Reese stopped abruptly when they passed through the doorway.

Reese looked from Taylor to Eliza. Although her lifestyle had taken a toll on Eliza, there was no mistaking the resemblance between the two women. Still silent, she glanced back at her grandmother before looking at Eliza again. "I know you. Mimi has a picture of you in her bedroom next to Auntie's. You're Auntie Taylor's sister."

Taylor forced herself to remain seated and not whisk Reese out of the room as Eliza smiled once again, revealing her missing teeth.

**

Taking a few steps back, he eyed the end cabinet he'd installed along the outer wall. Satisfied with the way it looked, he glanced toward the boxes containing the ones for the opposite wall. Did he want to start on those now or leave them until Monday? He hadn't even planned on working in the kitchen today.

When he set his alarm to wake him earlier than normal, he'd planned to tackle the next chapter in his book. Instead, he found himself working in the kitchen. Again.

All week his blank computer screen had tormented him. While it meant he got a lot of extra work done in the kitchen, it didn't get him any closer to the end of his novel.

He'd suffered writer's block before, but never like this. Usually a day or two away from his laptop while he engaged in some other activity fixed the problem. A whole week had passed, though, since he last typed a single sentence, and he'd engaged in plenty of other distractions.

This morning's failed attempt reinforced what he was beginning to suspect. No distraction was going to get his creative juices flowing again. Only coming clean with Taylor and getting rid of his guilt would.

In the beginning, he'd told himself he'd tell her the truth if and when he needed to. His gut told him the time had arrived. Unfortunately, it didn't tell him anything else—like how to go about doing it or what to expect for a reaction. Repeatedly, his cousin's words played through his head. *"You're asking for trouble. Take my word for it, women don't like secrets."*

He'd brushed off both his cousins at the time. Insisted it was no big deal. That everything would be fine. What a damn moron he'd been.

Curt grabbed the utility knife and sliced though the top of another box. Even if he knew how to start, telling her tonight wasn't an option. Both Priscilla and Reese would be there. Tomorrow was out as well. Taylor had mentioned taking Reese and her friend Hazel to an indoor trampoline park and then to the movies.

Monday. He'd ask her to come by after work. He'd explain that, while he was the author of *Fatal Deception* like he'd told her, his last name wasn't Hilton but Sherbrooke. He'd tell her why he'd kept the truth from her and answer any questions she had. Well, he would if she gave him opportunity. Honestly, Curt wasn't sure Taylor would stick around long enough. He could clearly picture her telling him to go to hell and walking out the door. It would suck if she did, because he cared about her. For him it wasn't all about the phenomenal sex, although it was a definite perk. A connection existed between them, one he suspected could easily develop into much more, given time.

He reconsidered his decision. The longer he waited, the worse it'd be.

"At this point, what's two more days?" He guessed he'd find out soon enough.

CHAPTER TEN

When he let Taylor and her family in several hours later he still hadn't gotten any work on the book done, but he had made significant progress in the kitchen. He considered that a Saturday well spent.

"Curt, we have Boston cream pie and two kinds of ice cream. Mimi and I made the pie from scratch." Reese held up the plate she carried for his inspection.

"Looks outstanding."

His comment earned him a beaming smile from the little girl. He'd learned over the past few weeks that it didn't take much to make Reese smile.

"And I brought my soccer ball. It's in my backpack. Can we go practice?"

His worries from earlier disappeared at her enthusiasm. Taylor had told him it was difficult to be upset with Reese around, and she was right.

"I told you not to nag him about that tonight." Priscilla followed her granddaughter into the house. The warm smile he'd come to associate with the older woman was absent. It was replaced by a subdued, forced one. "She wanted to bring the lacrosse stick over, too. I made her leave it at home."

Curt accepted the grocery bag containing the ice cream Priscilla handed him. "I'd love to practice soccer again, but how about after dinner? The steaks are already on the grill."

Reese took her backpack off and left it near the front door. "Mmm. I love steak."

Even with Taylor's mom and niece standing there, Curt couldn't resist moving closer to her and brushing his lips across her cheek. "I'm glad you're here."

"Me, too." She sounded and looked distracted. For a moment he wondered if she knew the truth about him. He quickly dismissed the idea. There was no way she'd figured it out from the guarded information he gave her. Something else was bothering her tonight.

He grasped her hand before he spoke again. "We're eating outside. If you want to head out there, I'll be there in a minute. Just need to put this away." He held up the plastic bag with the ice cream. "The quickest way out is down the hall and through the ballroom on the right."

Priscilla took the pie from Reese's hands and gave him a knowing look. "Take your time. I know the way out."

Taylor had mentioned that Priscilla and the previous owners were friends. He should've realized she'd been inside the house before today.

Once his other two guests were out of hearing, he turned his full attention on Taylor. "What's wrong?"

Her sigh could've knocked down a tree. "My sister made a surprise visit this morning."

He couldn't tell if she needed comfort or someone to vent her frustration out on. He decided to go with comfort, and wrapped his arms around her waist. "Were Reese and your mom there?"

Taylor nodded, the muscles in her jaw moving.

That explained the change he saw in Priscilla, too. "How'd it go?" It wasn't any of his business, but he cared about Taylor and liked her family. He didn't want to see any of them upset.

She closed her eyes and took a few deep breaths. "Let's talk about it later. I'd rather not think about it right this minute."

"You got it."

He held her hand all the way down the hallway, until they entered the kitchen.

"Wow, a little busy in here?" She looked around the room at the additional cabinets he'd installed since she'd seen it last night. "I thought you planned on writing today. What happened?"

Curt put the ice cream in the ancient refrigerator freezer, the only appliance still left in the kitchen. Since they all needed replacing anyway, he'd asked Ed to help him move the old dishwasher and stove out when he'd stopped over to help the previous week. He'd already ordered their replacements, as well as a new refrigerator. Hopefully, in another week he'd be ready for them to be delivered, because he was sick of washing his dishes by hand.

"Tried. Eventually, I gave up and worked in here." He opened a bottle of hard lemonade and passed it to her before opening one for himself. "What do you think your mom would like to drink? I picked up a red wine for dinner but can open something else now for her."

Taylor held up her bottle. "One of these is fine. And juice is good for Reese. If you don't have any, she'll drink water."

Curt grabbed another hard lemonade from the refrigerator, as well as a juice box.

"Didn't see you as a juice box kind of guy."

He didn't drink much juice himself, but he remembered drinking apple juice and fruit punch all the time at Reese's age. "I wanted to keep it a secret but"—definitely the wrong choice of words, considering the guilt pressing down on him already—"picked these up for Reese when I got the steaks."

She took her time surveying the room. "It's really

looking nice in here. I can't believe you got so much done today. Maybe this writer's block you have isn't the worst thing in the world."

"Tell that to my editor when I don't get the manuscript to her on time." He pulled out the macaroni salad he'd bought, along with the shrimp cocktail.

"Does it happen a lot? The writer's block."

"Once in a while." Did he need anything else? He went through a mental list of what he'd already set outside. "If you can carry the drinks, I'll take this."

She'd spent enough time in the house to know her way around, so she knew the quickest way to the back patio from here was through the kitchen's side door. "Anything particular cause it, or does it just happen?"

"Stress, exhaustion." *Guilt*. He wisely kept the last one to himself.

Taylor stopped walking, forcing him to as well. Her eyebrow arched, and he saw the spark in her eyes. "Maybe I should come by less often. Let you get more rest at night. Your editor would probably approve."

"Did I mention it's also caused by lack of sex?" He kissed the side of her neck. "We don't want to compound the problem, do we?" He whispered the question against her skin. "Don't worry, it'll pass soon." Yep, just as soon as he came clean with her.

***

Think about the positives, not your stupid sister. She'd told herself the same thing over and over since Eliza had left the house. Up until now she hadn't done a very good job of following her own commands. She'd give it another try, because there were a lot of positives around her. She was sitting outside on a gorgeous late spring evening. She'd had a delicious steak dinner with people she enjoyed spending time with. Reese looked over-the-moon happy, and it didn't appear as if Eliza's surprise visit had bothered her. Taylor wasn't sure if that was normal or not, but she'd concentrate more on the matter later. Last but not least in the "reasons to be happy" category was Curt.

She watched him steal the ball away from Reese and dribble it across the yard, her niece doing her best to catch him. The man had thought to buy juice boxes for Reese. How many other men without children of their own would think to do that? None. Or at least none she knew. If the guy was trying to win her over, he was doing a fine job of it.

"Reese and I should go soon," Mom said. She sat next to her, still nursing the last of her red wine. Unlike Reese, seeing Eliza today had bothered Mom. After Eliza left, Mom had gone upstairs. She hadn't stayed up there long, but when she came back she'd been unusually quiet as she and Reese baked. "Don't worry about rushing home."

"Are you sure?" She felt bad. Between her extra long days at work and spending time with Curt, it seemed Mom had been taking care of bedtime duty a lot lately. "I don't mind coming home with you guys."

Mom tipped her chin in Curt's direction. "I think he'd mind."

"Mom—"

"Hey, I'm not so old I don't recognize the signs. He's seriously interested in you. And my advice is to not let him get away." She winked at her. "If I'm not up when you come home, I'll see you in the morning."

Reese offered up a few grumbles when Priscilla announced it was time to leave. After Taylor reminded her of what she had to look forward to tomorrow, she conceded, and let Curt walk her and Priscilla to the car.

Taylor watched as Curt opened the car door for Mom. "Don't worry, I'll walk Taylor home," he assured Mom as she got behind the wheel.

She almost laughed at his comment, but managed to simply smile instead. She was more than capable of taking care of herself, and he knew it. "Reese, we'll have another lacrosse lesson soon."

Reese waved to them from the back seat as Mom

turned onto the street and then disappeared down their long driveway.

"Do you want to go in or stay outside?" Curt asked, taking her hand and leading her back up the stone walkway.

"It's too nice to be inside." She wished every night could be like this. It was the perfect temperature, and the humidity remained low. Even the mosquitos had stayed away so far.

They made a quick stop in the kitchen for more drinks. Unlike earlier, crickets provided the only noise around them. Taylor found the change soothing, especially considering the earlier events of the day. She'd blocked them out over dinner and dessert, and would prefer to keep them blocked out. Unfortunately, they were sneaking their way back into her thoughts.

"You're rather quiet." Curt's arm settled over her shoulders, and the warmth from his skin seeped into hers. "Do you want to talk about what's bothering you?"

"Yes. Maybe." She wasn't usually an indecisive individual. She rubbed the spot just above her eyebrow, more to give herself something to do than because it bothered her. "I'm not sure what to think, you know? Eliza hasn't stepped foot in the house since before her arrest, and then all of a sudden she shows up like she's been a regular visitor all along."

The hand resting on her shoulder moved, and he started massaging the back of her neck instead. "Did she give an explanation for her visit?"

"Some half-assed answer about wanting to wish Mom a happy Mother's Day." She rolled her eyes, even though Curt wasn't looking at her. "It's a lie, of course. Mother's Day isn't today. Even if it were, she could've called. Mom's had the same phone numbers forever."

"Why do you think she showed up?"

She hated admitting the truth, telling Curt her sister wouldn't think twice about stealing from her own family.

But she hated lying to him even more. If this relationship between them continued to develop, he needed to know what kind of people lingered on her family tree.

"Honestly, I think Eliza hoped no one would be home so she could break in and steal whatever she thought she could sell."

The hand massaging her neck stopped moving, and she waited for him to tell her he didn't need people with relatives such as those in his life. If he did she'd understand, too. Hate it, but understand, because she didn't want people like her sister in her life either. But as the old saying went, you can't pick your family.

"She'd do that to her mother? Her daughter?" Disgust and disbelief resonated in Curt's voice.

Taylor didn't want to see his expression, but she looked toward him anyway. "She's an addict. In my experience, they'll do anything to get money for another hit. That includes stealing from their families and sometimes worse." For the umpteenth time, she wished she could hunt down the person who'd first got Eliza hooked and kick his butt. "And I pretty sure she's done it before. Before my dad passed away, someone broke into my parents' house. Considering the things that were left behind, the only person it could've been was my sister. The police didn't get any useable fingerprints, so I can't be one-hundred percent certain."

"I'm sorry." His voice contained only sympathy. Before she could speak, he pressed his lips against hers. When he pulled away she saw compassion in his eyes, and nothing else. "How did Reese handle it? It was more or less her first time meeting her mom, right?"

He returned to massaging her neck, and at least one of her concerns slipped away. The additional information about her sister didn't seem to bother him. "Remarkably well."

Taylor wondered if she should contact the school's psychologist and inform her of this weekend's events.

She'd know better if Reese's reaction had been a normal one or something to be worried about. "Reese recognized Eliza right away. Mom still has her senior class picture in her bedroom next to mine. Eliza looks a lot older, but we still resemble each other."

Taylor thought back over Reese's behavior. Eliza hadn't stayed long, and soon after she left Reese and Mom got to work on dessert. Just in case either of them needed her she'd hung around the kitchen, but Reese never mentioned Eliza. She'd acted like the whole visit never happened.

"Reese never called her 'Mom.' When she saw Eliza, she said, "You're Auntie's sister." And then she went up to her bedroom. She showed no interest in Eliza at all. Do you think that's weird? I mean, she *is* her mom, and Reese knows it."

She felt the slight movement when he shrugged. "Maybe not. To Reese she's some random person who stopped by. There's no way she could have any memories of her. And you said Eliza's never contacted Reese. What does Priscilla think?"

"She's not sure either. We didn't talk much about it after Eliza left, but I know the visit bothered her a lot."

"Yeah, I noticed she didn't seem herself tonight. She barely said anything."

"I think she suspects Eliza came by for the same reason I do. She just doesn't want to say it." She hated they were spending their time together talking about family issues. At the same time, she appreciated Curt's willingness to listen, and his unbiased opinion.

"Understandable. It's her daughter. How'd you leave things with your sister?"

"Mom told her to call once in a while, and I asked her not to come back."

Curt chuckled. "You asked her? I'm not buying it. You might have worded it as a request, but your tone would've said something else."

He had her. "Either way, I can't shake this feeling she'll be back."

"Can I do anything to help?"

Some things in life you had no control over. Taylor knew this was one of them. "Maybe keep an eye out for any people or cars that don't belong around here. Other than that, I don't think there's anything either of us can do right now."

CHAPTER ELEVEN

Curt estimated he had a minimum of five hours. He'd never known Taylor to get home before five or after midnight. He hoped this Monday didn't prove to be any different. Even five more hours of pounding nails in the kitchen while at the same time mentally pounding his head into the wall, was almost more than he could handle.

He didn't know which bothered him more about the situation: The fact he still didn't know how to begin, or that he didn't know what her reaction would be once he did. When he asked her to come over right after work, she hadn't questioned his request. He suspected thoughts of her sister kept her too occupied to give his question any real thought. He'd been okay with that. Saturday night hadn't been the time to tell her the truth anyway. Eliza's visit had caused her enough stress and unease. Blurting out that he'd kept secrets from her would've caused more. Tonight might not be the best time to tell her either. She'd appeared more at ease when he walked her home, but who knew what emotions might be lingering today.

A nice long sit-down conversation later in the week might serve him better than one tonight. Curt considered it. Maybe he should gauge her emotions when she got here. If it appeared she'd had a stressful workday, he'd hold off. Tell her he'd asked her over just because he wanted to spend time with her. On the other hand, if she seemed relaxed, or at least relaxed for a Monday, he'd tell her everything. *And hope she doesn't tell me to go to hell.*

"I deserve it if she does." Curt wiped the sweat dripping down his forehead with the back of his hand. Then he swung the hammer, intending to drive another nail into the trim around the window. He missed.

"Fuck!"

Pain exploded in his thumb, and he shook his hand. First, he couldn't get rid of his writer's block, and now he was injuring himself. The hammer mishap wasn't the first time he'd hurt himself today. If he didn't get his head on straight soon, he ran the risk of either killing his writing career or himself. Neither were palatable options.

Screw it. Regardless of anything else, he'd sit her down and tell her the truth when she got here. And he'd start by first telling her he was sorry. He'd make sure to admit he'd been wrong, too, at some point during the conversation. In his experience, women liked when men admitted they'd been wrong.

Before his thumb blew up to the size of a tennis ball, he got an ice pack and called it a day. The risk of doing some permanent damage was too great. The kitchen would still be there tomorrow. Instead, he'd leave the ice on for bit and then play a video game. One of those didn't require much brain activity, just eyes and hands.

The sound of a car door closing reached him as he crossed the foyer. Although he had a good idea of the time already, he checked his watch. A little after noon. Way too early to be Taylor. Priscilla maybe? Did she need some kind of help? Had Eliza returned?

Curt pulled open the door and found Trent standing there, his index finger hovering over the doorbell.

"Still getting ready for your audition on *Left in The Wild*, I see," Trent said, in lieu of a proper greeting.

Skip the video games. Talking to his cousin didn't require much brain activity either. "What are you doing here?" He'd given his cousin his new address but assumed he would call before visiting, not show up on a random

Monday afternoon.

"I had a meeting in Lowell. When it finished, I decided to drive here. See how your new project is going. I'm guessing not good." He entered the house and pointed to the ice pack Curt held against his thumb.

Curt quickly glanced outside before he closed the door. Great. His cousin's Bugatti Veyron sat in his driveway. Trent owned other cars, including a Mercedes, which he usually drove when he wanted to go unnoticed, and a SUV for when he traveled with his wife and son. Why couldn't he have taken one of those today? No one would question either in his driveway. But a Bugatti would draw people's attention. Even people not into cars. At least it was the middle of the day. Most of his neighbors would be at work. Maybe no one would drive by and see the car.

"Minor accident. They go with the territory."

Trent checked out the library, the first room off the foyer. "Looks like the place has potential. How about a tour?"

They started upstairs and worked their way down. Curt intentionally left the kitchen for last.

"This looks familiar." Trent walked around the room. "Addie will be happy when I tell her you designed the kitchen after ours in Newport. She insists that's the best work she's ever done."

"Her layout and design fit this room well."

"It looks like you've spent a lot of time working in here. Getting anything done on the book?" Trent didn't ask before helping himself to a cola from the refrigerator.

Curt pulled out a drink for himself and leaned against the island that had been delivered. "Not even a damn word in over a week." He popped the can open and took a long swallow. "At this rate, I'll never get it finished."

"Writer's block, or something else keeping you from the keyboard?" Trent asked.

"Writer's block."

"How've you handled it before?"

"Different kind this time around."

Trent leaned against the island, next to him. "I didn't realize there were kinds." He took a sip from the can before he spoke again. "Is this kind related to the DEA agent you've been seeing?"

Leave it to Trent to know his writer's problems were related to a woman. Perhaps it was some kind of leftover benefit from dating so many women before meeting Addie.

"I think so."

"Bull. You know it."

He wanted to wipe the know-it-all smile off his cousin's face. He refrained. Trent had spent years practicing various types of martial arts and boxing. If Curt started a fight with him, even a friendly one, he'd lose and he knew it.

"What's the problem? Is she looking to get more serious than you want?" Trent asked.

"I plan on taking care of the problem tonight." So he hadn't answered Trent's questions. Big deal.

Trent laughed. "She still doesn't know who you really are, does she? Gray and I told you to come clean from the beginning. Now you're in deep and feel guilty, right?" He clapped Curt on the shoulder. "You should've listened to us."

"She's coming over after work. And, like I said, I'll explain everything then." Never would he tell Trent he'd been right. The guy was insufferable as it was. "It would be better if you were gone before she gets here."

"And miss the fireworks?"

"You'll have to wait until the Fourth of July for fireworks," Curt answered before he lifted his soda can to his mouth. Trent might bust his ass about it, but he'd never stick around and make the situation more difficult or awkward.

"What time do you expect her?" Trent asked.

"Not before five. Are you in a rush, or do you want to stick around? I was going to play the newest *Delta Force*

Recon," Curt said, referring to video game. A little company would pass the time and distract him from what he needed to do tonight.

"I haven't played the latest version. Yeah, I'll stay for an hour or so. I'll be out of here before five, though. Don't worry."

***

Taylor stopped at the red light and pulled out her cell to check for any new text messages. Even though he said he'd be home all day, she sent Curt a text when she left Conway to let him know she was on her way home. So far, she hadn't received any response from him. An unusual occurrence. He always got back to her. She tossed the cell back onto the passenger seat and accelerated when the light turned green.

She hadn't gotten home from work this early in a long time. After conducting interviews in Conway, it hadn't made much sense to drive back to Boston. Plus, she'd put in close to sixty hours the previous week. Her supervisor wouldn't mind if she cut this day a little short. Getting home on the earlier side also meant she could stop and see Curt sooner. Today she was more eager than usual to see him.

Yesterday, when he'd asked her to come over, he'd sounded different, sort of like he needed to discuss something with her. She'd lain awake thinking about it, too. First, she'd wondered if he intended to tell her it was time to part ways. Time to start seeing other people. That notion got dismissed rather quickly. A guy ready to dump you didn't invite you, your mom, and niece over for a cookout first. Unfortunately, with that idea off the table, she hadn't come up with any specific ones.

I could've imagined his tone was different. She drove through the rotary near the police station. Maybe he'd invited her over so they could spend time together without interruptions. He'd done it before, and then later come to her house for dinner.

Taylor stopped behind perhaps the most gorgeous vehicle she'd ever seen. She knew next to nothing about cars. Sure, she could identify the common makes and models, but there was nothing common about the low-slung sports car parked in Curt's driveway.

If he already had company, she should go home and come by later… but what she should do and what she planned to do were two different things. The investigator in her needed to know who owned the car parked outside Curt's house.

She guessed the expensive-looking car could belong to an author friend. Some well-known authors had millions in their bank accounts, thanks to record-breaking sales and movie deals. Since Curt was an author himself, it wasn't out of the question he knew some very well-known writers. The car could also belong to a client he'd met while working in the financial world. Heavy-hitting investors had more money than they knew what to do with.

Taylor slowed as she walked by the vehicle for a closer examination. Judging by the looks of it, the thing had to cost an easy six figures, if not more. While it was a gorgeous piece of machinery, she didn't think she'd pay that much for any car… regardless of her bank account balance.

Enough ogling. Time for some answers.

Curt answered moments after she rang the bell, his expression one of surprise and dread—a bad combination on anyone even him. Maybe his visitor was a woman. Did he have a girlfriend or wife he'd failed to tell her about?

"Taylor, you're early."

No hello? "I spent the morning up in Conway. It didn't make sense to drive down to Boston." She expected him to step back and invite her inside. When he didn't, she continued. "I sent you a text when I left the area, letting you know I was on my way here."

"Left my phone upstairs when I started work in the

kitchen, and I never bothered to go up and get it." Finally he stepped back and gestured for her to come inside. "C'mon in."

"Are you still working?" She doubted it, but maybe the car's owner knew a thing or two about remodeling homes and had come over to help. He had mentioned a friend named Ed who helped him out from time to time. Maybe Ed was a wealthy man with too much time on his hands.

After closing the door behind her, Curt gave her a brief hug and kiss. "No, I finished for the day. We were playing a video game."

It didn't escape her that he didn't provide a name for his guest. "If you have company, I can come back later." She tossed the ball into his court and waited.

Taking a step away from her, he pinched the bridge of his nose. "Stay. You can meet Trent." He gestured down the hall with his chin. "He's in the other room."

At least now the car's owner had a first name.

Since he didn't plan on tackling work in the ballroom for a while, he'd set up his living room in there. She'd noticed the various video game consoles hooked up when they watched a movie.

"What were you working on up in Conway?" Curt walked alongside her, but kept his hands loose by his sides.

"Interviews. The agency is working with the state and local police in the area on a case. I'll probably have to go back up sometime next week."

Curt's guest stood and put down the remote control he held when they walked into the room. Dressed in a pair of dark gray suit pants and a snow-white dress shirt with the top two buttons open, the guy looked like he was half ready for a business meeting. Considering who he was, she suspected he'd either just come from one or was on his way to one.

She'd seen Trent Sherbrooke on enough magazine covers and Internet sites over the years to recognize him anywhere. She'd always thought he was extremely handsome. However, seeing him in person, she knew the pictures hadn't done him justice. Especially his eyes. He, like so many in his family, had the most incredible shade of blue eyes. Eyes she couldn't tear her gaze away from at the moment. And not only because they were beautiful. No, she couldn't look away because she'd seen those eyes countless times over the past several weeks. Only, all those times the eyes had belonged to a different man.

Curt spoke first, breaking the awkward silence. "Trent, I'd like you to meet my girlfriend, Taylor."

He'd never used the term before, and after today she might not let him use it again.

"Taylor, this is my cousin. He was in the area and decided to stop in."

Billionaire Trent Sherbrooke was his cousin. No wonder Mom thought Curt looked familiar. Their next-door neighbor was Curt Sherbrooke, President Sherbrooke's nephew. The man had made more than one appearance on a magazine cover and Internet site himself.

"It's nice to finally meet you. Curt's told me a lot about you." Trent extended his hand.

Taylor looked from Curt to Trent and back again. His eyes should've clued her in long before now. That was probably why he'd always worn glasses, except for when they'd been in bed. Glasses he wasn't wearing now.

She shook Trent's hand. "Wish I could say the same, but he's never mentioned you. At least never by name." She went over as many of their conversations as she could and one popped out. "No, that's not true. He did tell me he had a cousin named Trent who worked for a big hotel chain." Talk about understating the facts. There were big hotel chains and then there was Sherbrooke Enterprises, one of the largest hotel chains in the world.

Wow, he played me for a fool.

"Since you have company, I'll go home. We can talk later." Curt had a lot of explaining to do, but she didn't need witnesses around when he did it. "It was nice meeting you, Trent. Curt, call me later." Before either man responded she turned and walked away, eager to get away from both.

Although she left the room before them, she only managed to open the front door and step outside when Trent and Curt reached her.

"Please stay," Curt said. He touched her forearm, but then pulled his hand away. "Trent is leaving."

"He's right. I've got a bit of a drive home." Trent smiled warmly at her. "I'm glad I got a chance to meet you." He fished his keys out of his pocket. "Sometime soon, you and my cousin need to join Addie, Kendrick, and me for dinner."

She ignored his comment about joining his family for dinner. Depending on what explanation Curt gave her, she may never see him again, never mind his family. "It was nice meeting you, too. Have a safe drive home."

An older model vehicle, its passenger side door painted a different color than the rest of it, slowly drove by, catching Taylor's attention. She didn't remember seeing the car around before.

"Tell Addie I said hello."

She heard Curt speak as she watched the car speed up and disappear from view.

Trent stepped outside. "Will do. Call me later."

The fancy car she'd admired a short while ago drove away, leaving her and Curt still standing on his front step.

"We need to talk," Curt said.

"You've a knack for understatement."

He touched her arm again, and slipped his fingers across her skin until he reached her hand. "Come back inside?" he asked as he gently squeezed her fingers. "Please."

She considered saying no. Making him wait and suffer until she was ready to hear whatever he had to say. Unfortunately, she didn't have the patience to wait. She wanted the whole story now, not a day from now.

Taylor stepped back inside and shook her hand free from his. She'd hear him out before she made a final judgment. However, for the moment he'd lost the right to touch her.

"How about we go in the other room? I think we'll be more comfortable." Curt closed the front door behind them then stuck his hands in his front jeans pockets.

With a simple nod, she walked back down the hallway. Curt didn't have much furniture in the house. It was either sit in his living room, his bedroom, or his office. His office only had one chair, and no way in hell was she going to his bedroom today.

"I know you've got some questions, but can I explain first?" Curt remained standing while she took the seat his cousin had been in before. "Afterwards, you can ask anything you want, and I'll answer you."

"As long as I get some answers, I don't care who goes first."

He ran a hand through his hair. "I didn't know my cousin would drop by. If I'd known you would be here so early—"

"You would've kicked him out sooner?" She'd agreed to hear him out first, but she couldn't keep the comment inside.

"Yes, but not for the reason you're thinking." He paced in front of her. "When I asked you over it was because I wanted to explain things. But having you meet Trent like that wasn't what I had in mind."

Her instincts last night had told her Curt wanted to talk about something. Revealing his true identity hadn't occurred to her as a possible discussion topic. Why would it? "Seeing him here was a little surprising." She was picking up his habit of understating facts.

He stopped moving and faced her. "I imagine it—"

"Doesn't matter now. Just tell me why you've been lying to me and my family since you moved in." His opinion on the situation didn't matter.

Curt let out a slow breath before he responded. "You've figured this out already, but my last name is Sherbrooke. Trent's one of my first cousins. He works for Sherbrooke Enterprises, my family's company. The bachelor party I went to a few weeks ago was for my cousin, Gray, one of Trent's brothers."

"Fascinating." Her annoyance grew with each passing moment. "But you didn't answer me. Why did you tell us you were Curt Hilton?"

"When I bought this house, I intended to keep to myself. I hoped no one around here would recognize me, and people would leave me alone while I worked. When I brought the cat home and Priscilla invited me for dinner, I thought it'd be a one-time thing. That afterwards we'd see each other in passing, nothing more."

"And then what happened? You decided to make up a story about being C.S. Hilton so you could come by for supper and get out of cooking your own meals?" She gripped both hands together in her lap instead of shaking him. *Can't the guy give me a straight answer?* she wondered.

"No, I *am* an author. I wrote the book under a pen name. Hilton is my mother's maiden name. You can probably guess why I don't use my real name for my books."

If a book came out with the name Sherbrooke on the front cover, it'd be a number-one best seller regardless of how well it was written. She could understand a person wanting his work judged on the quality of the writing and not by the author's last name. "Yeah, I can understand that. But considering we've had sex, you could've told me the truth."

He sat next to her, but his proximity only managed to fuel her frustration. Before he touched her, she stood and did some pacing of her own. "You should've told me. You've had plenty of opportunities before today, Curt. I wouldn't have told anyone."

"You're right."

"What?" Had he just agreed with her? Men didn't admit when they were wrong.

"I said, you're right." He sounded remorseful when he repeated his answer. "I should've told you weeks ago and not waited until now. My only excuse is that I wasn't sure I needed to. I figured if we only went out once or twice, you never needed to know. That I could go back to working on the house and my book. Then when I finished the renovations, I'd sell the house, move, and we'd never see each other again."

Somewhat an understandable excuse, even if she didn't approve. She stopped moving and faced him, her arms crossed over her chest. "And then your conscience got in the way, right? You decided to tell me now, so when you do move you don't feel guilty?"

"No." He stood and put his hands on her shoulders, making it difficult to move. "I needed to tell you because I care about you. I want to see what happens between us, and I can't do that if you don't know who I really am."

The guy was being honest now; she'd give him that much. She shook her head as the truth fully sank in. Billionaire Curt Sherbrooke, a guy who dined at the finest restaurants in the world, had been joining them for dinner and then playing soccer with her niece. She thought back over so many of the conversations they'd shared.

"Wow, what an idiot I am." She laughed sarcastically when one particular conversation about where his family members lived popped up, and the realization of who she stood there with hit her head on. It was either laugh or punch him in the nose. Laughing wouldn't get her arrested for assault.

"Your uncle is the president of the United States. He doesn't just live in Washington, D.C. He lives in the friggin' White House."

He grimaced. "Yeah, my uncle Warren is the current president. He's my dad's oldest brother."

Real laughter bubbled up. She wasn't sure what was

crazier: that he called the president of the United States, perhaps the most powerful man in the world, Uncle Warren, or that she'd been sleeping with the president's nephew. "And the beach house"—she made air quotes— "he owns, and you used to visit, is probably one of those gigantic mansions on the ocean."

"Yes, Cliff House is on Bellevue Avenue."

She'd toured some of the grand estates located along the famous street, so she had a good idea of what Cliff House must look like. "Jeez, how did I miss it? I should've realized you weren't who I thought you were. All the clues were right there."

When Taylor showed up much earlier than he expected, he wanted to strangle his cousin. Trent's presence made easing into the truth impossible. At least it was all out there. She hadn't shouted, attached any vulgar names to him, or slapped him. Yet.

All things considered, he'd take it and consider himself lucky so far, because she was pissed. If he stood in her position he would be, too. He just hoped she wasn't so mad she told him to get lost. Because when he'd said he cared about her, he spoke the truth. He cared a hell of a lot.

"Taylor, I'm the same person you've been spending time with." He might have kept his last name a secret, but he hadn't changed his personality. He hadn't done anything he wouldn't normally do.

"So I should just smile and forget you lied?"

"You have every right to be mad. I would be, too." He took her face between his hands. "But give me a chance to prove I'm who you thought I was. Prove that I care about you and your family. Please." She didn't move away. He took that as a positive sign.

"And what about Mom and Reese?" Taylor asked, her voice not giving much away.

"What about them?"

"Do you plan on telling them the truth, or do you expect me to keep all this from them?"

He'd not given it any thought one way or the other. If he hoped to keep Taylor in his life, he needed to be honest with her whole family. "Next time I see them, I'll explain everything. Or you can tell them tonight if you want."

"Right answer, buster."

"Does this mean you don't hate me?" He swallowed, and waited for an answer.

"It means I believe your explanation and understand it, even if I don't like it."

Taylor hadn't said she forgave him, but her answer was better than the other alternatives he'd envisioned.

"And because I care about you, I'm willing to give you another chance."

Relief washed over him and he lowered his lips toward hers. She'd given him what he'd asked for. Now he needed to make sure he didn't fuck it up, because he more than cared. Somewhere along the way he'd fallen in love with her. This wasn't the moment to tell her, though.

She anticipated his move and pulled back before he kissed her. "But no more lies or secrets between us. I won't be with someone who isn't honest with me. Got it?"

Meeting her demand wouldn't be a problem. "You know everything, Taylor. And I promise there'll be no more secrets. Ever."

"Then I think we're okay. But I should go." She kissed his cheek and moved farther away.

"Stay. It's still early."

She shook her head. "I want to change. I've had these heels on all day and my feet are done."

When she arrived, he'd been too preoccupied to notice her outfit. Now he took in the navy-blue skirt, matching jacket, and blue heels. He'd never seen her dressed in business attire. "Come back after. I can cook dinner on the grill for us. Bring your mom and Reese if you want. She can give me another soccer lesson."

The quicker things between them went back to the way they'd been before this chat, the better.

She appeared torn, so he went in for the kill. "I'll go over to the Java Bean and get a pie for dessert."

Finally, he got a genuine smile from her. The kind that made the dimple in her right cheek appear. "Let me check with Mom and Reese and get back to you. I don't know what Mom's plans are for tonight." She moved closer and kissed him. A brief press of her lips against his, but it still qualified as a kiss. "I'll let you know."

CHAPTER TWELVE

Taylor walked into an empty house. Even Stripes was lying outside on the back patio, soaking up the sunshine. A note on the kitchen table informed her Mom and Reese went to the grocery store and the mall but would be back before dinner. In her note, Mom mentioned sending Curt a text and inviting him over for dinner. Under Mom and Reese's names, her niece had added a large heart with eyes and a smiling mouth.

Just wonderful. Mom invited Curt for dinner.

She left the note behind and took her cell phone upstairs. At least having the house to herself gave her some time to think. To really process the bombshell Curt had dropped on her. For almost two months, she'd been living next to and dating billionaire Curt Sherbrooke. A member of the wealthiest family in America. A guy who called powerful politicians and business tycoons family. *Crazy.*

"His aunt and uncle live in the White House." Taylor spoke aloud as she walked upstairs. She still couldn't get her head around that particular detail. "How did I miss the clues?"

She considered herself a good investigator. She picked

up the little details most people overlooked. The more she considered their conversations, the more clues she realized he'd dropped and she'd missed.

Taylor left both her cell phone and jacket on her bed. Today's weather definitely called for a T-shirt and shorts, not pantyhose and heels.

The cell phone beeped as soon as she walked back with more comfortable clothes.

Priscilla invited me over. Should I say yes or no? the message from Curt read.

"At least he asked me first," she muttered.

Did she want him over tonight? Would waiting to see him again change anything? Make the truth any less odd? Nope. And she had already stuck her neck out there when she agreed to overlook the secret he'd kept. Even if she wanted to, she couldn't rescind her decision. She cared too much about him. As her mom had said weeks ago, Curt was a keeper. Perfect in every way, or at least he had been until today. Even in this instance, he hadn't so much lied to her as omitted details. He'd never once said he was Curt Hilton. Both she and Mom assumed as much when he said he wrote *Fatal Deception*. Everything he'd told her about his family was true; he'd merely failed to mention some of the finer details. Pieces of information she hadn't inquired about either, and maybe she should've.

She picked up the cell phone and typed back a message. *Say yes.*

A message immediately came back from him. *Okay. See you soon. I'll bring pie.*

She smiled at his message. Of course, a lot of the things Curt did made her smile; just one of the many reasons she was willing to move past his faux pas this one time.

***

"You're pulling my leg. It's not possible." Mom adamantly shook her head while she spoke.

What did she have to say to convince her mother? "Mom, I'm telling you the truth. Curt is a member of *the*

Sherbrooke family. Why would I lie about something like that?"

She'd decided to fill Mom in on everything before Curt arrived for dinner. So, right after they put away the groceries, she sent Reese outside to play and asked Mom to sit down. She'd expected Mom to be as shocked as she'd been. She hadn't thought Mom wouldn't believe her.

"And why would someone like Curt Sherbrooke buy the house next door? People like him live in Manhattan or Los Angeles. Maybe Boston. Certainly not Pelham, New Hampshire." Mom pointed in the direction of Curt's house, even though they couldn't see it from their kitchen. "The man living next door is an author. That's what he told us, remember? You and Reese were sitting right here when he did."

Okay, she'd try one more time. If Mom still refused to believe her, she'd leave it to Curt to convince her. He'd created the problem… he could solve it.

"I don't know why he picked this town, but Curt's not only the author of the book you love, he's President Sherbrooke's nephew. When I went to his house after work, Trent Sherbrooke was there. The two of them are first cousins, Mom."

The screen slider leading to the backyard screeched across the runner. "The president has a nephew?" Reese asked, stepping inside and catching the tail end of their conversation.

Even in the first grade, they talked about government and how the United States had a president, so Reese had a general idea of whom they referred to even if she didn't fully understand the role he played in the country.

"More than one. He has nieces, too." Taylor wasn't positive, but she thought he had two grandchildren now as well.

"Auntie Taylor, the president is too old to have nieces and nephews."

She had a good idea how Reese reached her conclusion.

"When I'm the President's age you'll still be my niece, won't you?"

Reese nodded.

"Then a person can have a nephew or niece no matter how old they are."

Reese considered the statement. "His nephew must be old like you."

To someone a few weeks shy of seven, thirty-four must seem ancient. "Yes, the president's nieces and nephews are around my age."

Happy with the answer, Reese said, "Mimi, are we eating soon? I'm super hungry."

Mom shot her a pointed look. "As soon as Curt is here, we'll eat. Why don't you go wash up so you're ready?"

Yep, Mom still didn't believe her. Oh, well. She'd learn the truth soon enough. She couldn't wait to see Mom's expression when she did.

"Do you think he'll give me another lacrosse lesson tonight?" Reese asked.

If Reese asked him, Curt would say yes. He'd never refused any of her previous requests. "Maybe. For now, go wash up like Mimi told you."

She skipped out of the kitchen. "Auntie Taylor, Curt's here." The little girl's voice traveled back into the kitchen. "Can I open the door?"

"Are you positive it's him?" Taylor asked, her mind instantly going to their unwelcome guest Saturday afternoon.

"I think so. He looks a little different, but it's his car."

I think so and *yes, I'm positive* were not the same thing. And a lot of cars looked alike. "Don't do anything. I'll be right there." Their visitor was probably Curt, but she'd rather verify it before Reese opened the door.

Through the front window, Taylor saw the SUV parked behind her car before she reached the door. Yep, it was his vehicle. *At least one of them.* Considering what she'd learned earlier, she wouldn't be surprised to learn the guy had a garage full of fancy cars like his cousin's somewhere.

"Go ahead open the door," she said.

The girl had the door open before Taylor finished talking.

"Curt, can we play lacrosse again?" Reese asked, rather than give the man a proper hello or allow him inside.

"I don't have my lacrosse stick with me, but if Taylor says it's okay we can play some soccer." He looked from Reese to her.

Reese looked her way, too. "Auntie Taylor, is it okay?"

She didn't see any reason they couldn't. "I'll even join you if you want. First go wash up for dinner."

The answer produced a huge grin and Reese raced upstairs, leaving them alone at the front door.

He'd changed his clothes since she left him. It wasn't the only thing he'd changed, though. His well-trimmed beard was gone, as were the glasses he usually wore. At some point since she left him, he'd visited a barber, too.

"You cut your hair." She took in the new him, or maybe this was the old him before he moved to town. Seeing him without the beard, shorter hair, and glasses, she wondered how she'd ever managed to mistake him for anyone other than billionaire Curt Sherbrooke.

Curt ran his free hand over his head. In his other hand he held two bakery boxes. "Couldn't take it anymore. I visited the barbershop over on Bridge Street right after you left. I never let my hair get so long."

"And you shaved." Talk about stating the obvious.

"Yeah, was getting a little tired of the beard, too." He held out the two bakery boxes. "As promised. One wild berry pie and one chocolate chip pie from the Java Bean." Curt dropped his voice to a whisper, and his gaze traveled over her face and searched her eyes. "I missed you." He moved closer, his nearness kindling a fire inside her.

Despite the topic of their last conversation, she'd missed him, too. "I'm glad you're here."

He gave her a dazzling smile, which left her wanting to

fan herself. "Have you talked with your mom yet?" he asked, his voice still low.

"Yep, and she doesn't believe me. She thinks I'm trying to pull some prank on her." Once Mom took one look at Curt tonight, she'd realize Taylor had been telling the truth.

Reese flew back down the stairs and joined them again before Curt commented. "Let's eat. I'm super hungry." She didn't wait for either adult before skipping down the hall for the kitchen.

"You heard her," Curt said with a chuckle.

Mom stood at the stove when they walked in.

"Curt brought dessert, Mom," Taylor said, anxious for Mom to turn around and see Curt's new look.

Priscilla set down the pan she pulled from the oven. "You didn't need to do…." Her voice trailed off when she turned and saw Curt standing there. "I thought Taylor was pulling my leg." She tossed her oven mitts aside. "From day one I thought you looked familiar, but I couldn't put my finger on it. Taylor thought maybe you reminded me of someone on television."

"Sorry I wasn't completely honest from the beginning, Priscilla. I hope you can forgive me."

What would Mom say now? Typically, Mom looked for the best in people and overlooked the mistakes they made. Lying, though, she'd always found harder to forgive.

"Let's consider it water under the bridge."

Curt glanced at each person seated around him. Other than Priscilla's initial surprise, none of the Walkers were treating him any differently than they had Saturday night or all the previous times he'd been with them. Even the mild aloofness Taylor exhibited this afternoon was gone, all good signs he hadn't ruined his relationship with her, something he'd worried about after she left his house. Time to think wasn't always a good thing, and she'd had plenty of it following their little chat. Tonight she'd greeted him with a smile and touched him every opportunity she got. Like now. After refilling both of their iced teas, she ran her hand across his shoulder before taking her own seat next to him again.

"I'm having my birthday party at Skate Kingdom. It's a roller skating place. Auntie Taylor already helped me write the invitations so we can mail them." Reese sat at the opposite side of the table. Much of her dinner remained on her plate because she'd been so busy talking. "If I give you one, will you come?"

She gave him the same look as when she wanted to play soccer. How Taylor and Priscilla ever told the girl no was beyond him. All she had to do was give him that look and the word okay slipped out of his mouth. This time he tried to restrain himself because a party inside a loud and crowded roller rink sounded damn close to hell.

"I haven't roller skated in a long time. I don't think I know how anymore."

"They have special skates. They make it easier, and I'll help you. So will Auntie Taylor." Reese looked expectantly at Taylor. "Will you help Curt at my party?"

"Curt probably wouldn't like Skate Kingdom. Maybe instead he can have dinner and cake with us, and you can just celebrate with your friends at Skate Kingdom." Taylor used her best diplomatic tone. He'd heard her use it before when addressing Reese. "We always take Reese out for dinner and let her pick the restaurant. After, we have cake here." Her hand slipped under the table and squeezed his thigh. He took the gesture as her way of telling him it was okay to say no to Reese this time.

Reese ignored her aunt's suggestion. "You'll love Skate Kingdom. They play music while you skate and sometimes turn on these special lights and your clothes glow. You can play video games, and we get to eat pizza."

"Pizza, huh? Does sound pretty great. Can I check my calendar and get back to you?" His request bought him a little more time.

"I'll get you an invitation." She hopped from her chair before anyone could stop her.

"You don't really have to go," Taylor said in a low voice, so it didn't travel outside the kitchen.

"I know."

Reese handed him an invitation decorated with pink soccer balls, the party details neatly written in, and then returned to her dinner.

"Thanks. And speaking of invitations, my cousin Trent called me right before I came over. He's having a cookout this weekend." When he'd seen his cousin's name, he almost didn't answer the phone. Considering what was going on when the guy left, Curt guessed Trent was calling to again say he should've listened to him earlier. Surprisingly, no such comment came. Instead, Trent invited him to a party in Newport.

"It'll only be family. A few of my cousins, my uncle Mark and his wife, and Trent's in-laws. We can all drive down on Friday when you get home, spend a few nights at my condo, and come home Sunday night."

Curt didn't think Taylor and her family would be comfortable spending the weekend at his cousin's house, even if there was room. And he wasn't sure there would be anyway.

"Won't your cousin mind a couple of party crashers?" Taylor asked.

"Nope. He specifically told me to invite you. When I mentioned Priscilla and Reese he said to bring them, too."

"It sounds lovely, Curt, but I already have plans for Saturday," Priscilla answered before Taylor could accept or decline. "But you and Reese go ahead. I'll be fine alone for a few days."

"Just family?" Taylor still sounded undecided.

He nodded. Trent hadn't given him a detailed guest list, but if Trent expected people he didn't consider family he would've told him. "It'll be fun."

"Okay. We'll come. I'll see if I can leave work a little

early on Friday so we can leave right after school."

"Will there be any kids?" Reese asked. She'd been silent on the matter so far, but her expression told him she'd heard and processed every word.

"Not your age. My cousin's son is only a year old."

"It sounds boring. Do I have to go?" Reese looked at her aunt. "Can I stay here with Mimi?"

Since he'd moved in, Taylor and Reese had become important to him. He wanted both to meet some of his family. "We'll have fun. My house is right on the beach. We can try to go swimming. Maybe build a sandcastle."

Reese didn't look convinced.

"If Reese really wants to stay home, I'll ask Leigh to come watch her while I go out," Priscilla said. "But going to Newport sounds like more fun than staying here with me."

Curt wasn't ready to concede the battle yet. "Pirate's Cove, the best ice cream and mini golf place anywhere, is in Newport. I'll make sure we go." He pulled out the big incentives. After all, what kid turned down mini golf and ice cream? "They've got batting cages and go-carts, too. I think you'll love it."

Reese scrunched up her mouth while she considered his offer. "Promise?"

"Promise."

Next to him Taylor listened, an amused smile on her face.

"Okay. I'll come. But I'm bringing Peanut."

Neither Taylor nor Priscilla said no, so he guessed Peanut wasn't anything living. Just in case Peanut turned out to be a pet mouse or snake she never mentioned before, he said. "Who's Peanut?"

"My tiger. I'll go get him, so you can meet him." Reese left the table, more than half her dinner still on the plate. It didn't take her long to return, a stuffed orange tiger in her hands. "This is Peanut. Auntie Taylor got him for me my first Christmas." She held the stuffed animal toward him.

"You can hold him."

Judging by the animal's condition, it was one well-loved toy. "Looks like he's your favorite." He accepted the toy, looked him over, and handed him back.

"Reese sleeps with him every night," Taylor said.

"Auntie Taylor won't let me take him to school." She took her seat and tucked the stuffed animal up next to her. "Can he come mini golfing, Curt?"

He'd once had a beloved stuffed animal. A brown dog he'd named Spot, though he didn't know why. The toy had been solid brown. He'd slept with it every night until he'd been a little older than Reese. If the thing had ever been lost or destroyed, he would have been devastated. Taking Reese's Peanut along to Pirate's Cove seemed like an ideal way for it to go missing.

"Sorry, Pirate's Cove doesn't let in tigers. Peanut will have to stay at my house. Maybe you could bring a friend for him to stay with, so he doesn't get lonely." Peanut couldn't be the only stuffed animal the little girl had.

Taylor squeezed his leg again and mouthed, "Thank you." Turning to Reese she said, "Curt's suggestion is a good one."

"Okay. I'm going to start packing." Reese slipped from her chair again.

"You've got plenty of time. You don't need to start now," Taylor said, stopping her niece in her tracks.

"But—"

"I need your help with dessert. I can't eat a whole chocolate chip pie alone," Curt said, hoping to distract the girl.

"We have chocolate chip pie?" Reese sat back down. "Can I have whipped cream on mine?"

***

Taylor came back outside and watched Curt dribble the soccer ball across the backyard toward the soccer net. Reese chased after him, trying to get the ball away. She almost succeeded, but at the last moment he moved to the left and she missed. Smiling, Taylor sat down in a patio chair. She'd played when they first came outside, but the phone call she just ended had pulled her away. Neither Curt nor Reese seemed to miss her, so while she could she'd enjoy watching them interact.

"Everything okay?" Mom asked. She'd followed them all outside after dessert, too. While Curt and Reese ran around, Mom worked on a crossword puzzle.

"Oh, yeah. Mary had a question about this morning's interviews."

Mom set aside her puzzle and watched the two players. "He's really good with her."

Mom would get no argument from her.

"I still can't believe he's Curt Sherbrooke," Mom whispered loud enough for Taylor to hear. "I really thought you were playing some kind of joke earlier."

Again, she couldn't disagree. She was still digesting the truth.

"I'm glad you didn't let his little fib ruin your relationship. I stand by what I said before. He's a keeper." Mom leaned closer and dropped her voice more. "And it's obvious he loves you."

She couldn't confirm or deny his feelings. But she did know hers. Even before today he'd captured a large part of her heart. Tonight, he'd breached the rest when he suggested Reese bring along a friend to keep Peanut company. How could she not love the guy after that?

Mom glanced at her watch. "Yikes. It's after eight." She gathered up her crossword book and empty glass. "Reese, time to say good night." She looked at Taylor as she stood. "Don't worry, I'll help her get ready for bed tonight."

"Just a little longer, Mimi. Please." Reese stopped in the middle of the backyard.

"Not tonight. It's after your bedtime already, and you still need a bath."

Reese gave the ball a hard kick and sent it flying into the net. "It's not fair. I wish I could stay up later." She grumbled but walked toward the patio, leaving the ball behind. Curt retrieved it and followed her over.

"I need go to bed soon, too." He dropped the soccer ball on the patio and sat next to Taylor.

"Can we play again this week?" Reese asked.

"You got it."

Reese hugged Taylor. "Good night, Auntie Taylor. I love you." She let go and put her arms around Curt. "'Night, Curt."

Taylor held her breath and waited for Curt's reaction.

As if he did it every night, he hugged Reese back then ruffled her hair. "See you later, short stuff."

Reese giggled. "That's a funny name."

If she hadn't loved him before, she certainly did now.

She waited until the slider closed behind them, indicating they were alone. "Are you sure you don't have children?" She hadn't intended to sound suspicious, but that's the way came out.

"No kids." He touched her cheek, and she instinctively leaned toward him. "If I had them, believe me, I'd tell you. I don't want any secrets between us."

"Neither do I." Choosing not to tell him she was falling in love him wasn't keeping a secret. It was more like withholding a final verdict until she'd gathered more evidence.

CHAPTER THIRTEEN

"Are we there yet?" Reese asked the one single question children had probably been uttering since the first horse-drawn cart was invented. Taylor understood. Long car rides got boring no matter your age. Even short ones could be annoying when you were eager to get somewhere. She'd made sure Reese took a book and her tablet so she could read or watch movies during the two-plus-hour drive. The book held Reese's attention until they hit the interstate. The movie had lasted slightly longer, and a short nap had filled in a good thirty minutes. She'd woken up over twenty minutes ago, though.

Taylor glanced into the back seat. "Almost." She guessed, anyway. They'd passed a sign welcoming them to the city of Newport. She'd visited only a handful of times, so she didn't recognize exactly where they were.

"Another ten minutes and we'll be at my house," Curt called from behind the wheel. Since he knew the route better, they'd taken his SUV. "We're going to stop for the pizzas Taylor ordered first." They passed the Tennis Hall of Fame, and he turned into a public parking lot. Pizza By The Court was right across the street.

"If you want to wait here, I'll be right back," he said.

Taylor had her door open before he pulled the keys from the ignition. "I put the order in my name. You wait. I'll get them." She left before Curt could mount an argument. The man hated to let her pay for anything when they went out.

True to his word, a short while later Curt punched in a security code and two massive gates opened, giving them access to a private residential community. She watched the gates begin to close after they drove through and waited for Reese to comment.

"Those are cool. How did you get them open?" Reese asked. She turned her whole body so she could peer out the back window. "Do you use a remote like the one for the TV?"

"If the guard isn't here to open it, I have a special code I type in," Curt answered. He drove them down the tree-lined road.

"Like Auntie Taylor uses to unlock her phone?" With the gates no longer in view, Reese turned around so she sat properly in her seat.

Special codes and security gates reminded her well with whom she rode. The man behind the wheel was not just some average Joe. She hadn't thought much about it since learning the truth Monday. Funny how something as mundane as a gate could remind you.

"Same basic idea," Taylor answered.

They passed two condos, or what he called condos. Actually, each looked larger than her house. He slowed as they passed a particular one. "My cousin and his wife live there."

"And that's where the party is tomorrow?" Taylor asked.

"Nope. Different cousin. Trent has a house on Ocean Drive. He's the one having the party. Derek lives here." He pointed toward the condo and kept driving. "Several of my cousins have homes in the area. At least for the moment, Derek and his wife, Brooklyn, are the only ones who live here full time. They'll probably be at the party tomorrow."

Curt drove past five equally beautiful condos before stopping at the final driveway. With the press of a button the garage door opened, revealing two vehicles parked inside. "How about pizza first? After that we can check out the beach. Or will it be too late?"

She tried to figure out what model of cars they'd pulled in next to. One resembled something she'd seen in a recent James Bond movie. The other was a complete mystery. Whatever they were, they belonged to Curt. She understood why he'd left them here instead of taking them to Pelham. Either of these vehicles would call attention to themselves.

"We should have time," she answered.

Taylor had left work early this afternoon and got home before the bus dropped Reese off. After Reese ate a quick snack and used the bathroom, they hit the road. Despite being a Friday afternoon, they'd made good time on the drive down. Assuming Reese didn't linger over dinner, they could take a walk on the beach and still get Reese into bed at a decent hour.

She carried the three pizza boxes inside, while Curt took care of all the bags except for Reese's backpack. The night before, she'd stuffed it with friends so Peanut wouldn't be lonely tomorrow when they left him behind. Peanut naturally hadn't made the backpack. Instead, he'd been strapped in next to her for much of the ride. The rest he'd spent on her lap.

"Make yourselves at home. I'll bring these upstairs and meet you in the kitchen." Curt left them standing in the entranceway and carried their things up the staircase.

"Let's find the kitchen." Taylor's comment gave Reese the go-ahead to move around and explore.

A room with a high ceiling took up much of the first floor. Glass doors lined the outermost wall, giving anyone in the room a perfect view of the ocean and beach. A large royal blue sofa faced two extra-large blue-and-white-striped chairs. Two dark coffee tables sat between the sofa and the chairs. Off to the right, a large opening led into an airy kitchen filled with windows. The barstools at the kitchen island matched the coffee tables in the living room. The whole place looked like it'd been plucked straight out of an interior-decorating magazine.

She placed the pizza boxes on the counter. *He told us to make ourselves at home.* She hadn't remembered to ask for paper plates when she picked up the food. The glass cabinet doors made locating plates easy. She took three of them down and left them near the pizzas. Glasses followed, although she didn't know what they'd drink. They hadn't brought any food or beverages with them, and he'd admitted he hadn't been at the condo in months. Why someone would have a place with a view like this and not come more often made no sense to her.

"Can I start eating?" Reese climbed onto a barstool and opened the top pizza box. "Yuck. This has sausage on it." She closed the cover and moved it out of the way.

"You know better, Reese Walker. We'll wait for Curt."

"No need. I'm here." He walked in and went straight to the refrigerator. "What do you want to drink, Reese? Looks like we have apple juice, lemonade, and milk."

"Apple juice," Reese answered, pulling open another pizza box for a peek inside.

Okay, how had he managed that? "Did you have a maid or someone go shopping for you?" The place appeared spotless. Not a speck of dust in sight. No house remained closed up for months and dust-free, too. It even smelled clean and fresh. Houses left empty for long periods of time got this stuffy smell to them. Curt's place smelled slightly of lemons and the ocean.

"Derek. Having a cousin as a neighbor comes in handy. I asked him to fill the refrigerator for me. He got us some hard lemonade as well." He twisted the caps off two bottles and handed her one. "Whatever we don't use this weekend, I'll get rid of when we leave."

She helped Reese get a slice of cheese pizza, her niece's favorite. "Did he clean, too?"

"He doesn't know one end of vacuum from the other. I called the service I always use to come in and touch things up. It handles the cleaning for most of the condos here."

She vacuumed and cleaned bathrooms because she had to. If she had access to a company that handled it, she'd call them in every week.

Dinner progressed much the same way it did at home. Reese gave them the full scoop of her day at school, and occasionally Taylor had to remind her to not only talk but eat, too. Later, they walked along the private beach she'd viewed from both the kitchen and living room. The ocean water lapping against her feet wasn't cold, but she needed the air temperature a little warmer before she went swimming in it. Neither Reese nor Curt seemed to mind the temperature. He held Reese's hand as they waded out far enough for the water to hit her knees before rolling back out.

Although still on the early side, only one other person sat outside enjoying the cool breezes off the ocean. Since Curt merely waved as they passed, she assumed the woman wasn't his cousin's wife. A few of the homes even looked empty. No lights appeared on inside, and at two of them the patio furniture on the deck remained covered up.

Before heading back inside, they walked the entire length of the beach in both directions. Reese managed to collect half a dozen seashells and watched the sky above them turn a gorgeous shade of pink as the sun went down. When the stars became visible, Taylor herded her niece inside and upstairs.

"Your bag is in here." Curt flipped on the bedroom light, revealing a room at least twice the size of Taylor's room at home.

"I get a TV?" Reese asked, her eyes wide. She walked

in, carrying Peanut and the backpack holding all of Peanut's friends. "What's in here?" She opened a closed door and turned on the light. "My own bathroom!"

Taylor went straight for the bag and searched for the toothbrush and toothpaste she'd packed. "And why don't we use it to brush your teeth." She handed Reese the items as well as her pajamas. "Change while you're in there, too. I'll wait right here." She closed the door and turned. Curt lounged in the doorway, his shoulder against the frame and his arms crossed.

"I put her in here so you'd be close by. My room is right across the hall." She must have made a face because he straightened up and moved into the room. "There's a third bedroom if you want it instead. Or you can stay in here, I guess."

She hadn't thought about sleeping arrangements when Curt invited them. Faced with the three options, only one appealed to her. "No, I'll stay with you. I'll just make sure I'm up in the morning before her."

Dating a woman with a child brought up issues he'd never considered before, like sleeping arrangements. The few girlfriends who'd stayed with him here or at one of his other homes always slept in his room. There had been no reason for them to sleep anywhere else. Taylor's hesitation made sense. Reese had probably never seen anyone in her aunt's bed. And despite her ability to carry on an intelligent conversation, Reese was not even seven years old, way too young to know anything about adult relationships.

"Okay, you've got Peanut and the gang. If you need me, I'll be across the hall. Just come and knock."

He watched Taylor pull the covers over Reese. The little girl clutched her stuffed tiger tightly. A stuffed penguin and a unicorn rested on the pillow to her right, while a stuffed white-and-black dog and an elephant rested under the covers on her left. He'd been surprised she'd managed to cram so many animals into her backpack.

Taylor hadn't blinked an eye when Reese pulled one animal after another from the bag.

"See you in the morning. I love you." Taylor kissed Reese's cheek.

Reese returned the hug. "Love you, too, Auntie Taylor." She let go and looked over at him. "Can I give you a good night hug, too?"

Before he'd realized it, she'd wrapped him around her little finger. Denying her anything, whether it was a soccer lesson, or in this case a hug, was now impossible. He came forward and took the seat Taylor vacated. What did people say when they tucked kids in? He tried to remember all the times his parents put him to bed.

"Sweet dreams, short stuff."

Reese kissed his cheek as she wrapped her arms around him. "'Night, Curt. I love you. Thanks for walking in the ocean with me."

He cleared his throat, trying to dislodge the golf ball stuck there. "Love you, too." Reese, much like her aunt, had crept into his heart and taken up residence there.

Taylor didn't comment on the words exchanged in Reese's room as they walked back outside. She must have heard their conversation. Reese wasn't exactly one to speak in a low voice, and Taylor had been standing close by.

"Between the TV in the room and the private bathroom, we might have trouble getting her to leave Sunday night. She's been asking for a TV in her bedroom for over two years. And even *I'd* love my own bathroom."

He'd brought a bottle of wine outside with them. Curt poured them each a glass and passed one to her as he listened.

"This condo is beautiful and the view incredible. I could get used to seeing this view every morning and night. I can't believe you don't live here year-round."

"The drive from here into Boston every day would've killed me. But I try to spend weekends here in the summer. I want you and Reese to come with me when I do." He sipped his wine and enjoyed the rich citrus flavor.

She didn't take a drink but instead set the glass down. "I heard Reese tell you she loves you." Taylor's fingers moved up and down the stem of the glass, her face a mask of worry and concentration. "And I heard your response."

Curt interpreted her worry immediately, but she continued before he had a chance to comment.

"I don't want her to get hurt." Taylor's voice contained an uncharacteristic wobble, something he never wanted to hear again when she spoke.

"I meant what I said. I don't know when it happened. Maybe when she started our soccer lessons. But I love her." Moving to the edge of his seat, Curt put his wine glass down next to hers. "I love her aunt, too." He spilled his heart out. It was her turn.

"Really? Do you know when that happened?"

Damned if I know exactly. "Maybe the day we put together my patio furniture. I asked you for an Allen wrench from the toolbox. Instead of asking what it looks like, you asked me what size I wanted. Other women I know would've either told me to get it myself or brought over the entire box because they didn't know what I was talking about."

"Well, knowing the difference between tools comes in handy. Imagine the disaster if the guy you love asked for a flat-head screwdriver and you brought him a hammer instead. He'd never finish renovating his house. He'd be stuck living there a long time because he couldn't sell it."

"I'm not really in any rush to finish. I enjoy doing the work and don't see myself selling the place anyway."

"Wasn't your grand plan to complete your book, renovate the house, and move on?"

Curt shrugged and reached for her. "Yeah, but when I made it I didn't know a sexy DEA agent who knew her way around a toolbox would be living next door. Now that I do, I changed the plan." He moved in, ready to kiss her.

"Change is good." She crossed the empty space

between them. "I'm glad you moved next door." Her last words were smothered against his lips.

Me, too. Her kiss made answering her verbally impossible. So he used his lips to show her instead.

CHAPTER FOURTEEN

While not as opulent and grandiose as the Gilded Age mansion along Bellevue Avenue, his cousin's home was more or less exactly what she'd expected. Located on Ocean Drive, the home sat on a piece of land jutting into the ocean. Sprawling green lawns spread out in all directions around the front of the home, providing a buffer between the house and the street. She could see at least three chimneys and various decks as Curt passed through the gates and down the driveway. They'd left all the vehicle's windows down, and the sound of crashing waves entertained them along the way, getting louder the farther they drove.

"Are you sure it's only family today?" She checked out the eight other cars parked around them, three with license plates from as far as Virginia. She recognized all the makes and models, even if she couldn't afford most of them. Two, though, didn't belong in the group with the others. The dark-colored pickup trucks, both with Virginia plates, stood out among the Mercedes and Porsches parked around them.

"Positive. Trent would've told me otherwise." Curt got out, then came around to open her door. "It doesn't look like my parents are here yet."

He'd never told her his parents would be here, too. She would've remembered a detail like that. "Your parents are coming?"

He closed the door Reese had left open when she climbed out. Eager for some exploration, she went off to check out the flowers near the garage. "I thought I told you." He sounded genuinely uncertain.

"Nope."

"Mom texted me Wednesday and said they'd be here."

She'd prepared herself to meet his cousins and uncle Mark. Meeting the guy's parents fell into a league all its own. Her boyfriend senior year of college had been the last one to introduce her to his parents. None of her relationships since then had even approached the level of seriousness that required an introduction to parents.

"Taylor, don't worry, they'll love you." Curt kissed her cheek and smiled. "Ready to go, short stuff?" he called out, before she answered or voiced her sudden apprehension.

An older woman with light brown hair and dark eyes answered the door. She didn't resemble any of the Sherbrookes Taylor had seen in pictures. However, dressed in tan-colored shorts and a floral print top, she didn't appear to be a staff member either. Curt confirmed her theory by hugging the woman.

"I was so glad when Trent said you were coming. I don't think I've seen you since New Year's," the woman said. She looked Taylor's way, a genuine smile spread across her face. "Trent mentioned you were bringing friends." The woman extended her hand. "It's nice to meet you. My stepson said you live next door to Curt."

Taylor matched the new pieces of information with what she already knew about the Sherbrooke family. If this was Trent's stepmother, then she was Mark Sherbrooke's wife. "Yes, along with my mother and niece. That's how we met." She wondered what other details Curt had shared with his cousin.

"Abby, this is my girlfriend, Taylor, and her niece, Reese." Curt finally got a word in. "Taylor, Abby is my uncle Mark's wife. Did Trent put you on door duty? Do you need me to set him straight for you? I'll go do it right now."

"He'd never do that and you know it. I was on my way upstairs when the doorbell rang. Everyone is outside. I'll be back down soon." Abby walked away, leaving the three of them in the foyer.

"This place is ginormous." Reese's voice sounded extra loud in the silence. She turned in a small circle, her head tipped back as she gazed up at the two-story ceiling.

Well, she's not wrong.

While the house Curt owned was large, it would fit into this one with room to spare. "Let's keep that comment to yourself." Taylor wished she'd gone over the type of comments Reese should try to refrain from blurting out.

"Don't worry about it. Both of you just have fun today."

He led them down a few hallways and finally stopped at a set of glass doors. On the other side, several people sat relaxing on the patio furniture, and she could see a few more guests on the sand. She put her hand over his before he pushed open the door.

"How about a quick run through of who's who out there."

"You met Trent already. The woman sitting next to him is his wife, Addie."

She'd guessed as much, but didn't interrupt him.

"The guy walking up from the beach with the baby on his shoulders is Trent's brother-in-law as well as my cousin Allison's boyfriend, Rock. The baby is Trent's son, Kendrick. Allison's not on the deck, so she must be down on the beach."

At least five people sat on the beach, and two of them were women. They both faced the water, making it impossible to see their faces and identify them.

"I'm guessing you recognize my cousin Jake."

Once referred to as Prince Charming by the media, she'd been seeing pictures of Jake Sherbrooke, the president's son, since she was a teenager. "Yep. He looks a little familiar."

Curt laughed. "Can't imagine why."

"And I'm guessing the redhead with him is his wife."

"Correct, Agent Walker. And the baby trying to wiggle down from Charlie's lap is their son, Garret."

"Since he's the president's son, shouldn't there be Secret Service agents lurking around? Last time I checked, the president's children got secret service protection while he was in office no matter how old they are."

"Who's the president's son?" Reese asked, letting Taylor know she was paying attention even if she didn't appear to be.

"My cousin Jake." Curt answered Reese first. "And he declined the protection right after Uncle Warren took office. Found it too intrusive."

"I'm not sure I'd do that, but okay." Put in a similar situation she'd probably opt for the protection, even if it meant someone looking over her shoulder all the time. "What about the ones at the table with the umbrella?"

"The man with the gray hair is Trent's father-in-law, Sal. Next to him is Trent's mother-in-law, Marta. Uncle Mark is sitting across from them."

"Got it."

"I saw Gray's car. He and Kiera must be down on the beach. Alec, too, because we parked next to his car."

"And who's the guy walking up from the beach now?" While handsome and around the same age as Curt's cousins, he didn't look anything like a Sherbrooke. Actually, he resembled the guy Curt called Rock quite a bit.

"Must be one of Addie's brothers. She has four. I've only met two, Rock and Jon. He's either Tom or Frank."

She stored all the names and faces away. "Besides your

parents, are a lot more people coming?"

"Beats me." He shrugged and opened the door. "Ready to formally meet the fam?"

Ready as I'll ever be.

Taylor's apprehension lasted for all of ten seconds after stepping out onto the deck. Immediately, Trent and Addie came over to welcome them. He proceeded to introduce her and Reese to everyone gathered on the deck before asking if they wanted anything.

"I thought you'd be here earlier. Did you drive down from New Hampshire this morning?" Trent asked when he came back with a bottle of juice for Reese and flavored water for both his wife and Taylor.

"We came down yesterday and spent the night at my house." Curt sat in a chair near his cousin Jake while Taylor sat next to him, Reese taking a spot on her lap.

"I had trouble getting someone out of the water this morning," Taylor added, twisting open her water after she helped Reese open her juice.

After breakfast, Reese had begged to go for a swim in the ocean. Taylor found the water a little chilly, but it hadn't bothered Curt or Reese.

"Did he throw one of his legendry temper tantrums?" Jake asked.

She caught the mischievous glint in Jake's eyes—eyes that were identical in color to Curt's—and she knew some embarrassing story must be on the way.

"We used to spend at least two weeks at Cliff House each summer. Every night before bed we were supposed to shower. Get all the sunscreen and stuff off. Curt would pitch a fit. Throw himself on the floor, roll around, and kick. He hated showers and baths."

If looks could kill, Jake would be dead. "Old age is causing you to be confused."

She didn't know Jake's exact age, but he didn't look much older than Curt.

"It was Alec who did that every night," Curt said.

Jake reached down and picked up his son, who decided he wanted someone's lap to sit in again. "Are you sure?"

"He's right. It was my brother who hated showers," Trent said, joining the conversation. "Curt threw tantrums when your mother made us eat whatever Henri prepared for dinner."

Jake snapped his fingers and nodded. "That's right. If Mom was there she'd make him sit at the table, even after we all finished and left, until he at least tasted what was on his plate. He fell asleep sitting there at least once."

A man who hadn't been on the deck when introductions were made stopped behind Jake's chair. "Are you talking about the night Curt face-planted into his plate because he wouldn't touch the vegetable on the side? One of the funniest things I've ever seen."

"No one asked you, Gray," Curt snapped.

Taylor giggled at the image of Curt falling asleep and landing face-first in his dinner. "Seriously, he fell into his meal?" While it'd make a funny scene in a movie, she didn't see it actually happening.

"When he pulled his face out he had this white creamy sauce Henri served with the meal dripping off his chin and nose," Gray said. "I think that was the last time he refused to eat what Henri served. Well, at least when Aunt Elizabeth was there. She was the only really strict one about that. And Aunt Marilyn never did it."

"I never fall asleep at the table. But I did fall asleep at the movies." Never one to be left out of a conversation, Reese jumped right in. "It was a boring movie."

"Boring movies put me to sleep, too," Gray said.

"And when he does you know, because he snores," Curt said, perhaps sharing some embarrassing information as a way to get even.

"Can I go play on the beach and build a sandcastle?" Reese asked. She'd asked about building a sandcastle both last night and this morning. Once she got an idea in her head, it didn't leave.

"There are already some buckets and shovels down there. I can show you where to change and then bring you down and make introductions. Alec, Allison, and Kiera are all still down there," Addie, Trent's wife, said.

She'd anticipated Reese wanting to hit the sand and water when they arrived, and planned accordingly by having Reese put her bathing suit on under her clothes. Since she didn't plan on touching the water, she hadn't packed one for herself.

"I already have my bathing suit on. See?" Reese lifted her T-shirt, revealing the black-and-white-striped bathing suit top underneath. "Can we go?" She bounced on the balls of her feet and looked at Taylor. "Please."

Not many things were more boring to a child than sitting around and listening to adults talk. "Sure."

He watched Reese skip ahead, Taylor and Addie following closely behind her. He hadn't been worried about whether or not his family would welcome them today. Even though none of them brought guests on a regular basis, he'd never known his family not to accept someone at a gathering. Taylor's comfort around them had concerned him, but judging by her interaction with his cousins so far, his concern appeared unnecessary. Too bad he couldn't say the same about his comfort so far this visit. He could've done without Jake sharing an embarrassing story the moment they sat down.

"Glad to see things worked out. I was worried when I left your house the other day." Trent picked up his son, who'd made his way over to him. "Still, you should've listened to me and Gray in the first place."

"What did our cousin do?" Jake asked.

Trent and Gray happily filled Jake in on all the details. Neither gave Curt a chance to get a word in and defend himself.

"Stupid idea, Curt. But it looks like everything turned out okay." Jake looked toward the beach, where Taylor stood talking to Addie while Reese began work on her sandcastle.

"And don't worry, we'll wait to tell her more stories about you some other time. Don't want to scare her away yet," Gray said.

Jake let his son climb from his lap back into Charlie's when she returned with a bowl of grapes cut up into small pieces. "We just need to get them all in before the wedding so she knows what she's getting ahead of time."

"Get what in before whose wedding?" Charlie asked.

"Curt's wedding," Jake answered.

Charlie's hand stopped, a grape almost to Garret's mouth, and she looked at him instead. "You're engaged? When did you propose?"

"No, your husband—"

Jake interrupted him before he finished. "You brought Taylor and her daughter to a family cookout. You've never brought a woman to a family-only event."

Except for when he'd introduced them to Abby inside, he hadn't mentioned Reese was Taylor's niece. Because of the close bond between them, most of the time he thought of Reese as Taylor's daughter. And Jake was correct. He'd brought dates to large fundraisers or events like the annual New Year's Eve party where hundreds of people would be around, but he'd never invited a girlfriend to a private family gathering like this cookout.

"Reese is her niece, not her daughter. Taylor's her guardian." He hoped his cousins didn't ask for more specific details, because they weren't his to share.

"Irrelevant. You still brought them with you today. A wedding's in your future, Cuz. Should I congratulate you today or wait until she has the ring on her finger?" Jake asked.

"He's ri—" Gray started but stopped, touching his forehead with two fingers and shaking his head. "Don't know if I can say this." He took in an exaggerated breath. "He's…." His voice trailed off.

"Right," Trent said, finishing the sentence for his brother. "I know. Difficult to comprehend, but Jake's right." He pretended to shudder.

They drove each other crazy and gave each other a hard time whenever they got the opportunity, but they also knew each other well. Jake, Gray, and Trent were right. He wouldn't have invited Taylor along this weekend if he didn't view their relationship much differently than any of his previous ones. And while he didn't intend to propose next week, he could see it happening in the future.

"Hey, he's right more than you think," Charlie said, dividing her attention between her son and the men. She'd spent enough time around them all to comfortably participate in any of their conversations, including those that involved busting each other's asses. "At least once every two months Jake is right about something."

"Not possible," Trent responded.

"I didn't say he was right about anything important," Charlie added, and from the tone of her voice she was really getting into the spirit of the conversation. "But usually if he says we're out of milk or Garret needs a diaper change, he's right."

Curt tuned out his family and focused on Taylor. Kiera and Allison had joined her and Addie. From here she appeared at ease, listening to his cousin's fiancée while Reese played a short distance away. An unexpected wave of tenderness washed over him at the scene on the beach. He started to walk away, his departure catching his cousins' attention.

"The SOB has it bad," Jake said.

"Yeah. Looks like Tasha's only got two Sherbrooke men left to go after," Trent said.

Curt didn't bother to stop and rejoin the conversation. Especially a conversation involving Tasha Marshall, a woman who'd been obsessed with Jake until he got married. Since then she'd tried to catch the attention of all Curt's male cousins, as well as him. And Trent was right.

There were only two Sherbrooke men now available: Brett, Curt's older brother, and Alec, his younger cousin. Everyone present knew Tasha didn't have a chance with either man.

***

They finished the first phase of the sandcastle, a large square structure with four round towers at each corner and walls connecting them together. In the center stood a fifth tower, this one taller than the other four, and a seashell was perched on top of it. Together they built a fifth wall, which would connect to the second phase of the castle. Reese insisted the second part be circular so that the horses could run around and not bump into any corners, because every castle had horses in it. He was working on smoothing out the sand so they could start the walls, when his parents stepped outside.

His dad, Jonathan Sherbrooke, was a slightly younger version of his two older brothers, Warren and Mark. So much so that anyone could easily confuse Jonathan as Jake's or Trent's father rather than their uncle. Following in both his father's and grandfather's footsteps, Jonathan studied business and joined the corporate world. He'd expected both his sons to follow suit. Brett, his oldest, never even tried. Curt hadn't thought twice about traveling the Sherbrooke path; at least not until he discovered he preferred life outside a suit and tie.

Dad wasn't happy when Curt broke the news that he'd left Nichols and the investment world behind. Business was the man's life. They hadn't spoken much since that unpleasant conversation. The last time they had, Dad tried to convince him he belonged in the world of high-rise office buildings and dollar signs. He hoped Dad didn't try again today.

On the other hand, Judith Sherbrooke, his mom, understood his decision. Although she came from a family entrenched in business, and had a law degree, she'd never practiced. Her true passion was art and music. She could spend hours sketching and painting, or wandering the halls of an art museum. He'd called her before anyone else when he learned his first novel would be published. Mom had also been the first to learn of his decision to leave Nichols and devote himself to his passions.

Regardless of everything else, both his parents were an important part of his life. He knew they'd both accept his decision to be with Taylor. With the exception of his recent career change, both had always supported and accepted every decision he'd made. However, he wanted them to like her, too, because he saw Taylor and Reese as permanent parts of his life.

He paused in smoothing the area intended for phase two. "My parents are here."

Taylor put down the shell she held. She and Reese were using shells to make a walkway from the middle tower to an outer castle wall. "Did you tell them Reese and I would be here?" She glanced toward the house.

Curt nodded. When Mom texted him, he'd replied with a message of his own. Mom would've shared the information with Dad. "Of course." He put the shovels they'd been using into a bucket. "How about a break, short stuff? We can finish this up later."

Reese didn't even look up from what she was working on. "Do I have to?"

All the times they'd been together, Reese had never refused one of his requests or suggestions. He wasn't sure how to respond to her question. Thankfully Taylor stepped in, taking care of the problem for him.

"This isn't going anywhere. Come on. Let's go, Reese. Curt wants us to meet his parents."

Her sigh probably reached his family members on the deck, but she stood up and brushed some sand from her knees.

The message he'd sent Mom merely said he was bringing his new girlfriend and her niece. He hadn't included how they'd met, or how long they'd been together. All he'd shared was their names. Always one to show affection no matter the company, Mom immediately embraced him and kissed his cheek. A little more reserved, Dad didn't like public displays of affection no matter if it was just family around them or not. Instead, he gave Curt a thump on the back and a "Good to see you again."

"I'm glad I get a chance to meet you today. Let's sit and chat. I want to make sure my son's been behaving himself and treating you properly," his mom said once he finished making introductions.

"Curt's teaching me to play lacrosse," Reese said. "And I'm giving him soccer lessons. And tomorrow he's taking Auntie Taylor and me to Pirate's Cove. I can't wait to play mini golf. I've never played. He says I'll like it."

Mom looked at him, one perfectly curved eyebrow raised, as Reese continued to talk her ear off. He interpreted the look easily. She knew how serious his relationship was and wanted to know why she and Dad were only now meeting Taylor. He shrugged. What else could he do? It was either that, or admit to her he'd tried to keep his identity a secret. Unlike his cousins, Mom would never understand his actions.

"That sounds like so much fun. I wish I could go. I've never played mini golf either," Mom said, leading Reese and Taylor toward three patio chairs, leaving him alone with his dad.

Mom played golf regularly, but he couldn't picture her anywhere near a mini golf course.

"How long are you staying in Newport?" Dad asked.

He stopped trying to picture Mom hitting an orange golf ball into a windmill and headed for some empty chairs. "We'll head back tomorrow night. Reese is still in school and Taylor has work."

"Speaking of work. I saw Jim Burke at the club recently. He wanted to know what it would take to get you to come back. You've had a nice break. Maybe you should reconsider and give him a call."

Up until this moment, the day had been so relaxing. "Not interested, Dad."

"Really?" He sounded baffled by the prospect of anyone turning down the life Jim Burke represented. "You're satisfied living in New Hampshire, writing books, and working on an old house?" He shook his head. "It's great to have hobbies or things to do outside the office, but is that how you want to spend the next twenty or thirty years? Wouldn't you be happier living in Boston again? Meeting me and Mark or Harrison at the club for a round of golf?"

Dad didn't sound upset, merely confused. A definite step up from their last conversation. "No."

Dad rubbed his chin. Curt guessed his father worked at digesting the response he'd given. "When do you think you'll finish the renovations and move back to Boston?"

Never. "I see no reason to move back." He looked toward Taylor and his mom, chatting away like two old friends. Between them, Reese sat enjoying a slice of watermelon. "Everything I want is in Pelham."

CHAPTER FIFTEEN

Taylor checked her cell phone again. No text messages or missed calls. Good. She forced herself to slip the device back into her purse before she called home a second time. She'd called this morning not long after sitting down at her desk. Mom had assured her everything was fine at home. Everything was okay at work. Curt sat next to her, so he was fine, too. None of that mattered, because her gut told her something different. She couldn't explain it or shake the unease that had been bouncing around inside her since she got out of bed this morning.

"Are you still with me?" Curt asked.

They hadn't planned on meeting for lunch today. Or, at least she hadn't planned on seeing him for lunch. He arrived at her office building at noon, a picnic lunch in hand. Now, they sat on the same park bench they'd used back in April.

She pinched his arm. "If you felt that, I'm still here."

"Could've fooled me. You haven't said a thing since we sat down, and I just asked you a question. Is something wrong?"

I hope not. "I don't think so. But all day I've had this feeling like something is wrong or going to be wrong. Ever get that?"

"Once in a while, but it passes."

He put his arm over her shoulders. Usually the gesture made her feel loved and cared for. Today, unease overpowered any other emotions.

"Did you call home?" He'd come to know her so well since moving in next door.

"This morning. I talked to Mom before she left for the library. And I haven't gotten any calls from her or anyone else."

Curt gently squeezed her upper arm. "Then I'm sure everything is okay. Priscilla would call if it wasn't."

He's right. Mom called even if she had to pick Reese up from school because she was sick. If Mom couldn't get through, she always left a message letting her know. "You're right. Sorry. What did you ask me?"

"I need to get a birthday present for Reese. Do you have any suggestions?"

"Not really. She wants to take guitar lessons, so Mom bought her a child-sized guitar. And she wants a scooter, so I got that. Maybe ask her. I'm sure she'll think of something, even if it's just another stuffed animal. Peanut can't have enough friends, you know."

"I really doubt Peanut needs more friends. I've seen his entourage."

"Try telling her that."

"I did have one idea. How about tickets to see the New England Revolution play?" Curt asked, referring to the professional soccer team. "I checked the website before I left, and the next home game we could make is in July."

His suggestion required no consideration. "She'd love that. Her soccer team went last year, but she missed it. Strep throat. To say she was disappointed would be an understatement."

"I'll order tickets tonight. Maybe I'll get Peanut a friend, too, so she has a present to unwrap next week. What do you think about a zebra? I haven't seen her with one of those."

"I don't think she has one of those." Considering all the stuffed animals in Reese's bedroom, it was difficult to know for sure. "But don't quote me on it."

A cell phone beeped, letting its owner know they had a message, and Taylor pulled out her phone. "Not me."

Curt took his phone out. "It's Peter, my realtor." He typed back a short message and set the cell aside.

He said he had no intentions of selling the house. Is he looking for another project? His current one isn't even close to being halfway done. Has he decided to give up on it and move on? "Plan on buying something else?"

"No. Selling." He picked up the phone again when it beeped. After reading the message, he put it back down.

"The house too much for you?" She'd suspected the place needed more work than one person could handle alone.

"Nope... selling my condo here in the city. I see no reason to keep it."

She'd never seen his condo in Boston, but he'd mentioned he kept it even after moving in next door. "Guess that means we're stuck with you next door, huh?"

"Get used to it. I'm not going anywhere."

Taylor leaned in and kissed him. "I'll find some way of dealing with you over there."

Another beep disturbed the quiet around them. Curt peeked at his cell phone on the bench. "It's not mine this time."

The sick feeling in her stomach grew as she pulled out her phone. The message wasn't from Mom, but her coworker Mary. "Sorry. I hate to cut lunch short, but I need to get back to the office. And depending on how this problem goes, it might be a long day."

***

The new development in a case kept her mind busy and pushed everything else into the background, at least until she left the city and started home. Unfortunately, no distractions kept her occupied during her commute. Not even any traffic required her attention as she made the routine trip back. Most nights she considered having the road mostly to herself a perk of working late. Tonight she could've used the distraction her fellow drivers provided.

Mom's home, and Reese is in bed sleeping. She pulled onto her street. If they were anywhere else, Mom would've called. When she walked in the door, Mom would probably be watching television or reading a book. Reese would be tucked in upstairs, Stripes mixed in with the various stuffed animals cluttering her bed.

Taylor passed Curt's house. No lights showed, but that didn't mean he wasn't working. His office was located at the back of the house. Before leaving her after lunch, he mentioned writing tonight. With two more chapters to finish before he started his revisions, he hoped to get them in before his cousin's wedding this weekend.

Light spilled out of all the windows downstairs, indicating Mom was up and about. And like whenever Taylor worked late, Mom had left the light at the front door on.

The scent of peanut butter and chocolate welcomed her inside. Judging by the aroma, Mom and Reese had spent some time baking after school. Whatever they'd made was probably for tomorrow's end of school year party.

End of the school year already. Taylor shook her head in denial. How could Reese already be done with the first grade? Wasn't it just the other day she'd been changing her diapers and helping her learn to walk? Now, she could ride a bike and read bedtime stories to herself. Before Taylor realized it, Reese would be asking to borrow the car for a date.

"Really late tonight." Mom walked into the hall. She'd changed for bed, but the reading glasses perched on her nose said she hadn't been asleep.

Taylor pulled out her hair elastic and undid the tight

braid. "Tell me about it. We got some new leads at lunch, and they took longer than I hoped to look into." Around three she'd sent Mom a text, letting her know she'd be on the later side tonight. She hadn't thought she would be this late.

"We saved some dinner for you."

"Any chance you saved whatever smells so good, too?" She found the idea of something sweet much more appealing.

"Reese put aside a few cookies. The rest are for tomorrow's party at school."

"Great. Are you heading up to bed?" She started down toward the kitchen, her nose following the scent of chocolate.

"Not just yet. I'll sit with you while you eat."

The hair on the back of her neck lifted. Occasionally, when she got home after Reese went to bed they'd sit and chat while she ate, but not usually this late.

"Is there something we need to talk about?"

Mom removed her glasses and left them on the table before putting a covered plate into the microwave.

"Mom?" She was keeping something from her.

Still silent, she brought over two glasses of iced tea. "Eliza came over today."

Anger and annoyance joined the apprehension churning inside her. "When? Was Reese home?"

"This afternoon. Right before Reese got off the bus." Mom sat down and fingered her eyeglasses.

"Why didn't you call me?"

"Your message said you were working on something important and would be late. I didn't want to bother you."

Even if Mom had called, there wouldn't have been anything she could do. Without a time machine, she couldn't do a damn thing about it now either. "What did she want this time? Money?" After all this time, none of them needed her back in their lives... especially Reese.

"No. At least, she never asked me for any. She didn't

say a whole lot to me except she wants to get to know Reese."

Mental red flags sprang up. *Hell no. Not happening in this lifetime.*

"Most of the visit she spent with Reese. They played a board game. Don't worry, I stayed in the room with them. She helped us make the cookies for the school party. She left before dinner."

After more than six years, Eliza wanted to get involved in Reese's life? Taylor wasn't buying it. Her sister had another reason for coming around again today.

"What did they talk about?" Taylor asked, needing to get to the bottom of this.

"School mostly. Her birthday next weekend. And Reese talked a lot about the weekend she spent in Newport with you and Curt."

"Anything else?"

The microwave beeped again, reminding them the food was done. This time Taylor didn't ignore it. She removed the dish of pasta but left it on the counter, her appetite long gone.

"Reese talked about Jamie's birthday party this Saturday."

Big surprise there. She'd been talking about her friend's upcoming party since she opened the invitation.

"You don't believe Eliza?" Mom's question sounded more like a statement.

"Do you?"

She slumped in her chair. "I want to. But no. I don't either."

Taylor rolled the information around, trying to pick out a clue or two. Nothing pointed to Eliza's real reason for visiting again. Maybe she'd missed a hint or detail.

"How did she get here?" Public transportation in town was nonexistent. She didn't know where Eliza called home these days, but she didn't think it was within walking distance.

"Her boyfriend dropped her off, and came back later. He never came inside." Mom actually rolled her eyes when she answered. If they weren't discussing such a serious topic, Taylor would've laughed.

"Great." They both knew they type of men Eliza spent her time with. "Can you describe the car?" Maybe the boyfriend had Eliza scouting out homes they could break into.

"An older car with four doors. It was a dark color. Either black or blue. The emblem was missing from the front."

"Was the front passenger side door a different color?" She'd kept an eye out for the car she'd seen driving by weeks ago, but so far hadn't seen it again.

"Funny you say that. The passenger door was white."

Yep, sounded like Eliza and her boyfriend were scouting the neighborhood. Tomorrow she'd call the town police and give them a heads-up. It might not stop her sister, but there wasn't much else she could do.

***

The end. Curt typed the words and rubbed his eyes. Done. He'd finished with more than enough time to do revisions before sending the manuscript off to his editor. More importantly, he'd finished before his and Taylor's trip to Newport for Gray's wedding, meaning he could enjoy himself without the stress of knowing what awaited him at home.

Rolling back his office chair he stretched his arms over his head, and his stomach rumbled. After leaving Taylor at her office, he met with Peter briefly and came straight home. His ass had been in his chair ever since. He'd only left it for bathroom breaks and to refill his water bottle. It had to be late. He'd turned the desk light on a long time ago.

Midnight. He checked his watch to confirm what the clock on his laptop said. Even later than he thought. Tomorrow, he'd pay for sitting in one place for so long.

He saved the manuscript to a thumb drive before shutting down the computer, something he did every time he wrote. He'd learned the hard way the importance of not only backing up his computer once a month on an external hard drive, but also saving his story on a secondary device every time he added to it or made changes. Of course, since he'd started using the thumb drive he'd never needed it.

In an attempt to avoid distractions, he left his cell phone in his bedroom. His laptop in bed for the night, he stopped there first before heading down to raid the kitchen. With his mind no longer engaged, his stomach demanded he feed it, making sleep impossible.

A quick peek at the screen showed he'd received two messages: one from his mother regarding the wedding this weekend, and one from Taylor telling him she'd just gotten home and good night. She sent him a similar message whenever she worked late, at his request. While she'd never take any unnecessary risks, she worked in a field that required she carry a firearm every day. If Curt didn't see her, he at least liked to know she was home safe and sound.

He checked the time on Taylor's message. Ten o'clock. She'd expected a late night after the message from her coworker this afternoon, and she'd been right.

Had her subconscious been right, too? He hoped she would call him if something was wrong at home. She knew how much he'd come to care for both Priscilla and Reese. They'd come to be family to him. If they needed anything, he'd be there for them the same way he would for his own family. Tomorrow he'd make sure she knew that.

His refrigerator offered him few choices. An almost empty gallon of milk and some sliced turkey were the only two things inside. Between renovations and the book, shopping had taken a back seat this week. With the weekend a day away, a trip to the grocery store didn't seem worth it. He wouldn't be around to eat anyway.

Tomorrow, when Taylor got home, they'd leave for Newport and three nights alone. He'd enjoyed their last trip down with Reese, but he was looking forward to having Taylor all to himself. Except for the wedding ceremony and reception Saturday, there'd be no distractions or responsibilities for either of them. And he planned to take full advantage of that.

CHAPTER SIXTEEN

I'm at a wedding with the president of the United States. Despite their suits and ties, the Secret Service agents stood out among the guests, reminding her just who was somewhere inside the mansion.

She watched the agent currently standing near a door into Cliff House. Sunglasses covered his eyes, but she suspected he took in everything around him, making sure the president remained safe while attending his nephew's wedding. She would never want the agent's job. She preferred knowing who the bad guys were and being on the offensive, rather than having them surprise her. Another agent, this one a woman, approached the one Taylor watched. They exchanged a few words then the female agent entered the mansion, a building she'd only gotten a brief look at inside when they first arrived. As she expected, Cliff House was as extravagant and grand as the Newport mansions open to the public for tours.

While inside, she had met a few more of Curt's cousins, including the president's daughters, Callie and Sara, and their husbands. Honestly, neither woman had needed introductions. She would've recognized both women and their spouses anywhere. But that had been well over an hour ago, long before many of the other guests arrived.

Taylor felt his presence before she heard his voice. She always did. Whenever he was near, the air around her changed. Her body picked up on his proximity. Taylor couldn't explain it.

"Sorry I was gone so long."

"I didn't even realize you'd left."

Curt touched her back and slowly caressed the skin exposed by the dress. "Is that so?" He left a trail of goose bumps behind. "Guess I need to work harder tonight when we get home, so you don't forget about me so easily in the future."

She thought about how hard he'd worked this morning after waking her up. Liquid heat exploded in her stomach. If he worked much harder, she'd be dead. But she would certainly die happy and with a smile on her face.

"I bumped into Derek on my way back. He invited us out on his boat tomorrow afternoon."

Taylor pulled her thoughts out of Curt's bedroom and back to their conversation. A safer place for them, considering the number of people gathered around them. "What did you tell him?" She'd gone on a cruise once, but otherwise she'd never stepped foot on anything bigger than a kayak. A day out on the open ocean sounded fun.

"Some other time. It's only June. We've got all summer, and Derek and Brooklyn go out all the time. I think my cousin would live at sea if he could."

His cousin was Derek Sherbrooke. The man never needed to step foot in a courtroom and represent a client again. Like all of Curt's relatives, he had more money than he'd ever need. Oddly, none of them acted that way. At least none of the family members she'd met so far did.

"It would make getting a pizza delivered difficult," Taylor said, rather than what she'd really been thinking. They never discussed money, and she avoided the topic of his family tree.

"That's not the only downside, trust me. I spent two

weeks out on a boat with Derek a few summers ago. Two of the longest weeks of my life."

Yeah, not being able to get a pizza did sound insignificant compared to the difficulties she imagined living at sea could create.

She spotted Jake walking toward them before Curt did. She'd guessed he was around somewhere, but this was the first time she'd seen him today. "I think your cousin is looking for you." Taylor touched his arm while she spoke, and he followed her gaze.

"I hate to be the one to tell you this, but Nana wants the photographer to do a picture of all the grandchildren together before the wedding," Jake said after greeting them. "Uncle Mark sent me to round up you and Scott. Everyone else is already in the library."

"You're kidding."

"Curt, does it look like I'm kidding?" The first time she met Jake, she noticed he had a sense of humor. Right now, though, he sounded completely serious. She didn't think he was pulling Curt's leg.

"Aren't we all a bit old for family pictures?"

"Nana's almost ninety. Do you really think she cares how old we are?" Jake asked.

She'd met Curt's grandmother when they first arrived. The woman didn't look or act like any ninety-year-old women she knew.

"She said the one she's got is too old. And since everyone's here today, including your brother, she wants a new one. The sooner we go, the sooner it'll be over," Jake explained before Curt protested more.

Holding in her laughter was impossible. Listening to the two grown men complain as they walked across the lawn reminded her of Reese's response when told to clean her room or put away her laundry. "Think of it like this: you'll be making your nana very happy."

Her comment earned her a dirty look from both men.

"I see Scott with Aunt Marilyn. I'll grab him and meet

you inside," Jake said before leaving them.

From the doorway, she watched the photographer position everyone before stepping back and surveying the group. Taylor thought it looked perfect. Evidently the photographer disagreed, because she directed Curt and Scott to swap places then asked Curt's sister to turn more to the right.

"No. No. Gray should stand between Derek and Trent," Theresa Sherbrooke, Curt's grandmother, told the photographer. Just one of half a dozen suggestions she'd given since they gathered together in the library.

Before she lost it and disturbed everyone with her laughter, Taylor moved into the hallway. She was quickly learning Curt's grandmother was a force all her own, as well as a woman with the love and respect of her entire family.

An unexpected ring sounded from her purse. She'd brought her cell along in case an emergency came up at home. She never actually expected to hear it ring today, or even this weekend. Taylor took several more steps away from the library door before pulling it out.

Mom. The simple name stared back at Taylor as a sudden coldness descended over her, sinking into her very core. She leaned against the wall and swallowed. Mom knew her plans for today. She'd never call unless an emergency had come up at home. "What's wrong?" she demanded, skipping a polite hello.

"Reese is missing." Mom said the words Taylor prayed she'd never hear. "Your sister took her."

Fear welled up inside her chest and choked her. No matter how hard she tried, she couldn't get enough air into her lungs. Her heart hammered against her chest, threatening to break through her rib cage. *This can't be happening.*

Get it together, Taylor commanded. She needed a clear head. Without one, she'd be of no help to Reese or Mom.

"Eliza took Reese? When? How?"

"This afternoon, from the birthday party." Mom confirmed Taylor's worst nightmare.

"Did you call the police?" It didn't matter if Eliza was Reese's biological mother or not. If she'd taken Reese without permission, the police needed to be involved.

"They're with me now." Mom's voice quivered.

She wanted every detail, but first she needed a way home. "Let me find a way home and I'll call you back. If anything changes before you hear from me, call right away."

Asking Curt to leave his cousin's wedding was out, which left her with two options: borrow Curt's convertible, or use Rent-A-Ride. She'd rather drive herself, but understood Curt not wanting her to borrow a car that cost more than some homes.

With the family photo done, many of Curt's cousins had left the library, including those in the wedding party. She'd lost track of time, but the ceremony must start soon. She didn't pause before walking inside. Ignoring all the manners Mom drilled into her over the years, Taylor interrupted Jake, who stood talking with Curt.

"I need to go. If you don't want me to borrow your car, I understand. But I wanted you to know I left." She pulled up Rent-A-Ride's app on her phone and turned away. Time wasn't on her side. She needed to arrange a ride and get on the road. Her family needed her.

"Wait. Hold on." His fingers closed around her wrist. "What happened?" he asked, his voice calm and concerned at the same time.

She looked up from her phone long enough to answer. "Mom called. Eliza took Reese. I need to get home." Taylor kept her voice low. Everyone in the library, including Jake, didn't need to know Eliza kidnapped Reese.

"Let's go. I'll drive." He glanced back at Jake, who looked curious, but she couldn't tell if he'd overhead her or not. "Tell Gray I'm sorry. We've got an emergency and need to leave."

Jake nodded, a solemn expression across his face. "Will do. Call if we can help."

Taking her hand, Curt led her down several halls and out a side door in silence.

"Are you sure about this?" she asked before getting into his car. "This is your cousin's wedding." She'd seen firsthand how close he was to his family. She hated being the reason he was about to miss it.

Usually, he opened her door and closed it once she got inside. Not now. Instead, he left her standing there and walked around to the other side. "Jake will let Gray know what happened. He'll understand. Get in."

Curt started the car before she closed her door. He had them off the estate and on the road moments later.

Summer weekends always drew crowds to the area. Today was no different. While Curt navigated the busy streets, she called Mom back for an update and more details.

The muscles in his forearms quivered, and he relaxed the death grip on the steering wheel. Next to him, Taylor remained on the phone. So far much of the conversation was one-sided, so he knew little more than what Taylor had told him before they left. Taylor's sister had kidnapped her own daughter. What kind of a sick person did that?

"If she calls or brings Reese home, call me." Taylor put the phone down and rubbed both hands down her face.

"What happened?" Priscilla might allow her eldest daughter into her home, but she'd never leave Eliza alone with Reese.

Taylor leaned her head against the seat, her eyes closed. "Reese went to a friend's birthday party today. Reese has gone to parties at this pottery studio before. The area used for parties isn't very big, so they encourage parents to drop kids off and come back. That's what Mom did." She looked across at him. "Jamie and her family moved to town this year, so Jamie's mom didn't know Eliza isn't in Reese's life. She told Mom Eliza showed up and said she was picking Reese up because Mom had an emergency. Evidently, Reese called Eliza by name and seemed okay about leaving with her. Jamie's mom had no reason to think Reese couldn't leave with Eliza."

"Christ. How'd Eliza know she was there?"

"When Eliza came over Thursday, Reese told her all about the party she was going to this weekend. You know how she talks. Mom didn't think it was a big deal, so she didn't try to stop her."

Who would? They'd called the police, and he assumed an Amber Alert had been issued. But situations like this called for all the manpower possible. Curt handed Taylor his cell phone. "Go into my contacts and bring up Eric Coleman for me." He prayed they got home and learned the police had found both Reese and Eliza, but he didn't plan to wait and see if it happened.

"Uh, okay. Why?" She scrolled through his list of numbers. "Who's Eric Coleman?"

"The director of Elite Force Security."

"And what's Elite Force Security?"

Talk about a loaded question. "Originally, it was a firm that provided private security to anyone who hired them. My family has used them many times in the past. Over time they've branched out into other areas. They often handle high-profile kidnapping situations. The firm only employs the best. If the police can't find them, Elite Force will."

Taylor passed the cell phone back to him. He pressed the green icon on the screen and waited for Eric Coleman, the firm's director, to answer.

The call was short, and after, they both remained silent, lost in their own thoughts for the rest of the long trip.

When Curt pulled in, a police cruiser and two other vehicles were parked behind Taylor's and Priscilla's cars. Since Taylor received no phone calls on the drive, he knew none of them had brought Reese home.

They'll find her. Thinking about Reese alone with Taylor's sister scared the hell out of him, and he wasn't even related to her. He could only imagine what it did to Taylor and Priscilla.

"Mr. McIntyre is here." Taylor opened the door before he shifted the car into park. "He's chief of police in town. He and Dad joined the force together. He probably came over to check on Mom."

Explained who one car belonged to anyway. Curt followed her inside the house.

An older gentleman dressed for a day on a golf course stood behind Priscilla, his hands on her shoulders. Two FBI agents, their badges and firearms visible, sat at the kitchen table. One had a phone to his ear while the other had a laptop open. A uniformed officer completed the gathering in the kitchen.

"Good. You're home." Priscilla's voice broke, the only sign of her distress. If Taylor hadn't shared everything, he'd never know by looking at Priscilla that something was wrong. He noticed the same about Taylor. Throughout the ride, he'd expected Taylor to break down. To cry or yell. She'd remained dry-eyed and in control the whole time. It appeared as though Priscilla shared her daughter's strength.

Priscilla quickly made introductions.

"Anything yet?" Taylor asked.

"No," Priscilla answered. She reached up and covered Mr. McIntyre's hand with hers. "Not yet." The small gesture made him wonder if Mr. McIntyre was more than a family friend.

Smack. The sound of flesh coming down hard on wood filled the room. He saw Priscilla jump. Whatever leash Taylor had on her emotions was coming undone.

"What the hell is being done? Eliza has no money. No resources. And let's face it, she's not smart. How far could she have gone?" With each word Taylor's voice grew louder, more evidence the stress was wearing down her control.

Curt rested his hands on her shoulders, her skin ice-cold beneath his palms. Wanting to offer some comfort, even if it meant simply keeping her warm, he took off his suit jacket and draped it over her shoulders.

"Miss Walker, believe me, we're following every lead we get," one of the FBI agents answered. He proceeded to explain each step they'd taken so far and answered every question Taylor threw at him. "We've also been contacted by Elite Force Security. My supervisor informed me they're assisting with the investigation."

"Eliza won't harm Reese," Priscilla said. Her unspoken words hung over the table. Eliza wouldn't intentionally harm Reese, but that didn't mean she wouldn't do something that would put her in danger. Considering the woman had a history of drug abuse, anything could happen before the authorities located them and brought Reese home.

***

Taylor reached the bookcase, turned, and walked back. How was it possible less than six hours had passed since Mom called her? "This is—"

"It's not your fault." Curt didn't let her finish. "Priscilla blamed herself when you were upstairs. And it's not her fault either. Neither of you could've known Eliza would do this."

He'd only left her side once since they returned home, to change his clothes. She appreciated his presence more than she could ever tell him.

"I don't get it. What is my stupid sister thinking?" None of it made sense. Since giving up custody, Eliza acted like she'd never given birth to a child. So why all of sudden did she disappear with Reese? What had changed? What did she want?

Taylor gave up on pacing. Maybe sitting in one place would help her figure out her sister's motivation.

"She did come around a few times. Is it possible she

wants to be involved in Reese's life again?" Curt asked. "Could this be Eliza's way of doing that, because she thought you wouldn't let her spend time with Reese?"

She'd considered and immediately dismissed the same thought earlier. Whatever ideas prompted Eliza's actions today, being a loving mom had nothing to do with them. "No. Even before I became Reese's guardian, Eliza wasn't interested in being a mother. She left Reese with Mom or me every chance she got. She did this for some other reason. I just can't figure out what."

Taylor heard the house phone ring. No one ever called the landline anymore. They'd even considered getting rid of it rather than pay for something they never used. *Let that be Eliza or Reese. Please.*

Mom got to the phone before she did. "Please let me talk to Reese," Mom said, her voice shaking. "Just to say hello, so I know she's okay. I'm her grandmother. I need to know she's okay."

Taylor stood near the kitchen table and wished she could hear both sides of the conversation.

"Then let me talk to Eliza. Is she there?" Mom asked in desperation.

Great. Reese wasn't only with Eliza, but also whatever scumbag Eliza spent time with these days. But why wasn't Eliza calling herself? Had something happened to her since leaving the pottery studio with Reese? Had Eliza left Reese with someone? A friend even more screwed up than her?

The color drained from Mom's face. "Yes, I understand, but…."

Taylor gripped the edge of the table.

"I don't…." Again, whatever Mom intended got cut off by the scumbag on phone. "Okay. She's here." She passed the phone to Taylor. "He wants to talk to you." Mom covered her face with one hand, and Mr. McIntyre reached for the other. He'd been there since Taylor came home, constantly offering Mom reassuring words or holding her hand.

Across the room, one of the FBI agents sat with headphones on so he could hear both sides of the telephone conversation. He met Taylor's eyes and nodded.

She cleared her throat and licked her bottom lip, her mouth suddenly dry. "Hello. Who is this?" Taylor demanded. She wouldn't let the caller or Eliza know the toll this was taking on her.

"A friend of your sister," a male voice answered. "And if you want your niece back, Taylor, you'll do what I say."

She pushed aside her anger and hatred. Neither would do any good at the moment. She'd let both emotions have free rein when her sister and this jerk were tracked down and arrested. "I'm listening, but I want to talk to my niece." She heard loud music in the background, but nothing else to help pinpoint what type of place he called from.

"You only need to listen. It's easy. Get us a million dollars, and we'll give you Reese. Don't, and she stays with us."

She'd seen people do unspeakable things, first as a police officer and then a DEA agent, but she never thought Eliza would kidnap and ransom her daughter.

"There is no way I can get you that much money. My sister knows it's not possible. Let me talk to her."

A sick laugh assaulted her ears. "Eliza and I know you're fucking Curt Sherbrooke. We think you should share your good luck. Go ask him for it. He won't miss it. I'll call you back."

The line went dead.

She let the scumbag's words sink in. Money. This was all about money.

"What did he say?" Curt asked.

"They want money in exchange for Reese."

Mom nodded, and she wiped a tear from her face. "Okay. How much? The bank is closed until Monday, but maybe if we contact the branch manager and explain they'll open up. I'll clean out my accounts."

Even if they both cleaned out all their accounts and Reese's college fund, they'd never have enough.

"One million."

Whatever strength Mom had relied on so far today gave out. Sobs wracked her body and tears fell uncontrollably down her face. Before Taylor could attempt to comfort her, Mr. McIntyre wrapped his arms around her.

"But… that makes no sense," Mom said between her sobs. "I'm not surprised they want money. But one million! That's crazy."

Grinding her teeth, she pulled on whatever reserves of strength she had left. For both Mom's and Reese's sakes, she had to keep it together. After, when they had Reese home safe, she could fall apart. "He'll call back."

"How can Eliza do this? She knows we don't have anything close to a million dollars. It doesn't make any sense," Mom said, her voice almost a shout.

Considering everything else, it was the only part that did make sense. "Somehow they know Curt Sherbrooke lives next door. They also know I'm in a relationship with him." No need to repeat the crude language the caller used. "They're hoping we can get the money from him." She'd think about how Eliza had learned Curt's identity some other time. Mom wouldn't have shared it with her, and Reese didn't comprehend the significance of who he was.

"When and where?" Curt asked without a word from her. He already had his cell phone out. "It'll take a little time for me to get a million in cash."

Taylor doubted Eliza and her boyfriend, or whoever the scumbag was, would want anything but cash. A wire transfer to a bank required the receiving party to have an account. Drug addicts who kidnapped children didn't seem likely to have an account at the local bank. And no one simply walked into a bank, cashed a million-dollar check, and walked back out with a briefcase full of hundred-dollar bills without calling attention their way.

"He didn't say. All he gave was the dollar amount," she answered.

"Mr. Sherbrooke, before you agree to meet the—" the agent who had listened to the entire phone conversation began.

"Agent Torre, I'll do what I need to." He reached across and squeezed Mom's hand before he took hers. "Don't worry. We'll get her back." Curt called whatever contact he pulled up and walked away.

I hope. Paying Eliza and her boyfriend didn't guarantee they'd get Reese back. Everyone there, even Mom, knew it.

***

The backyard light let her see Curt standing on the patio while he talked to his cousin. Taylor didn't blame him for taking a break and going outside. The tension inside had become a tangible thing, weighing on them all, making her anxious and worried one moment and angry as hell the next. She'd thought about escaping the house and tension off and on all day by getting in her car and searching for Reese and Eliza herself. The fact Eliza's boyfriend hadn't called back yet was all that kept her from putting her plan into action. He'd insisted on talking to her and not Mom the first time. When he called again, it made sense he'd do the same thing. She couldn't afford to miss his call.

"You look exhausted. Maybe you should try to get some sleep," Mom said, coming back into the kitchen alone.

"I think you need it more than me. Did Mr. McIntyre leave?"

"He'll be right back. He needs to let Petey out. The poor dog has been inside all day. I'm making some tea. Do you want some?"

She didn't remember the last time she'd had anything to drink. "Sure." Outside, Curt started pacing; she wondered how much he was sharing with whatever cousin had called him.

"How do you think Eliza learned Curt was a Sherbrooke?" The car with the mismatched door that she saw pass Curt's house the day Trent made his surprise visit had to be the same one that dropped Eliza off the last time she came over. Eliza and her boyfriend would've seen Trent's expensive sports car parked in the driveway, but there was no way for them to link it back to a Sherbrooke.

Mom filled the teapot, the one Reese had picked out as a gift one Mother's Day, and put it on the stove. "Maybe after Reese told Eliza about her trip to Newport she got curious. She could've gone to the town hall and asked who owned the house next door. Sonia Anne works in the town clerk's office. She and Eliza were friends in high school. She might have helped her out. There's also a database on the town website. If you put in any address in town, it'll tell you who owns the property. Curt's full legal name would've come up."

"Yeah, but would she have thought to do any of that?" Her sister spent much of her time either high or looking to get high. Could she carry out a plan like Mom theorized?

The teapot whistled behind her. "Maybe." Mom poured the hot water into two large mugs. "Or her boyfriend may have known to check with the town hall." She added sugar to both mugs before bringing them over. "I think this whole thing was his idea. Eliza wouldn't do this on her own. Not to her daughter. Her boyfriend put her up to it."

Maybe at one time she would've agreed, but the woman who'd dropped in weeks ago wasn't the person Taylor had grown up with.

"I have to believe that," Mom said softly.

If thinking Eliza's boyfriend forced her to kidnap Reese helped Mom get through this situation, she'd let her believe it. Convincing her otherwise didn't change the facts or bring Reese home any sooner.

The door from the backyard slid open, and Curt

walked inside. "Jake wanted me to tell you hello. He called to see how everything was and ask if he could help."

Had Jake overheard her in the library? She'd tried to keep her voice as low as possible. And Curt had merely told Jake they had to leave because of an emergency.

"Does he know what's going on?" Taylor asked. She'd rather Curt's entire family not know all the details.

At the stove, Curt made himself a cup of tea. She hadn't seen him eat or drink anything in hours either. "No. He knows you have a family emergency. He doesn't know the specifics. I didn't think it was any of his business."

The cordless phone on the counter rang, and every set of eyes locked on it.

Like earlier, Agent Torre slipped on headphones and gave her a thumbs-up.

"Hello," Taylor said, in a clear controlled voice.

"Do you have our money?" Eliza, not the scumbag from earlier, asked.

Her sister's voice gave her pause. Could she reason with Eliza? Get her to bring Reese home tonight? *Maybe when hell freezes over.* Mom might put all the blame on Eliza's boyfriend, but she didn't buy it. Eliza had played a role in what happened today.

"Let me talk to Reese," Taylor said. She needed to hear her niece's voice more than she needed air. Eliza might at least give her that. "I need to know she's okay, Eliza. You can understand that."

Taylor heard what sounded like music in the background, then nothing. Did Eliza hang up?

"Auntie Taylor." Reese's voice knocked the breath out of her. "I want to come home."

Her throat closed up, and she couldn't speak at first. "Are you okay?" Reese didn't sound scared, merely bored. The last thing she wanted to do was scare her.

"I'm bored and I want Peanut. I miss you and Mimi. Eliza says Mimi is sick and I can't come home until she's better. Is she better yet? It smells funny here. I don't like it."

Maybe if she kept Reese on the phone long enough, she'd get some useful clues about her whereabouts. "Don't worry, Mimi is okay. Do you know where you are? I'll come and—"

"You talked. Do you have what I want?" a man's voice came on the phone, cutting off her sentence.

Damn. She didn't get to tell Reese she loved her. "We're working on it. No one keeps that much money hanging around their house."

"I want it by Monday. Meet Eliza outside Faneuil Hall with the money."

"Will Reese be with her?"

"Be there at ten and come alone. No police".

CHAPTER SEVENTEEN

Thud. Curt's head hit the end table, the sudden impact waking him. He blinked and took in his surroundings. He sat on the sofa in the Walkers' living room. Taylor leaned against him, her head on his shoulder, sound asleep. Priscilla slept in the chair across from him. Her head was tipped back and her mouth slightly open, while Stripes slept curled up in her lap.

He lifted his head as the events of the past day and night rushed back. Eliza and her boyfriend had Reese and were demanding money. How long had it been since the two assholes contacted them? Had the authorities made any progress in finding them? What about the security firm's HRT, hostile response team? Honestly, he had more faith in them than anyone else working the case. Unlike the police and FBI, the members of the HRT didn't have to follow a strict chain of command. The firm gave them a lot of leeway when handling situations in the field.

Against him Taylor moved, the comforting warmth of her body disappearing. "I didn't mean to fall asleep. What time is it?" Sleep clung to her voice. He knew she needed more rest but would never willingly take it.

He checked his watch. "Almost four." They'd been out for two hours. Curt rolled his head, his neck stiff from sleeping in an upright position.

191

Taylor yawned and stretched her arms over her head. "I should be out there doing something. Not sitting here and napping," she said with annoyance. "Poor Reese probably cried herself to sleep. She hates not having Peanut at bedtime. She cries if she has to go to bed without him."

"Reese will be okay." He kept telling himself the same thing. "Forcing yourself to stay awake won't help. I just woke up, too." He reached over and rubbed her neck. Considering her sleeping position, she probably had a stiff neck as well. "Even your Mom is catching a nap."

"That's different."

She sounded angry with herself. He'd tried convincing her earlier the situation wasn't her fault. His argument then had fallen on deaf ears. If he tried now it probably would, too, but he'd give it a try.

"Why? And don't say because this is your fault. It's not."

"Mom works in a library. She doesn't deal with people like my sister and her scumbag boyfriend every day. I do." She moved away toward the edge of the sofa and turned back to look at him. "I know the types of places they use. I should be out searching for them, not waiting for the phone to ring."

He understood her sense of helplessness. The same one filled him. Running around aimlessly wouldn't help Reese or the authorities. "Taylor, I know you're frustrated. I am, too, but we don't know where to start. They might not even still be in New Hampshire." Massachusetts was only a short ten-minute drive away. Parts of Maine could be reached in less than an hour, too.

"It doesn't matter. I can't sit here."

When she stood, he knew he'd lost the battle, but he wouldn't let her go off alone. "I'll come—"

Taylor's cell phone on the end table rang, and a cold fist punched through his chest and grabbed his heart. The authorities wouldn't give bad news over the phone, he reminded himself, passing the device to her. Bad news, they'd deliver in person.

She answered the call, and before she finished her greeting his cell phone rang. Two calls so close together couldn't be a coincidence. He checked the screen. *Eric Coleman.*

Curt skipped a greeting. Considering the circumstances, the firm's director would understand. "Eric, tell me you have good news."

"HRT found her."

Elite Force Security wasn't cheap, but it never disappointed. He'd been right to call them.

"Connor, the team leader, is coordinating with the police and FBI. Once they have a plan, they'll go in and get her," the firm's director explained.

Eric's comment somewhat diminished Curt's happiness. When the director said they'd found her, he'd thought Eric meant the team physically had her. That Reese was safely away from her bitch of a mother and the deadbeat with Eliza.

"How long until she's home?" Curt asked.

"Matter of hours. When I hear back from Connor, I'll contact you again. Sit tight. This will be over soon," Eric assured him with confidence.

Easier said than done. The little girl meant a hell of a lot to him.

Taylor and Curt ended their calls about the same time.

"Agent Morris says your security firm found Reese and Eliza." Taylor referred to another FBI agent assigned to the case. "They're holed up in an apartment in Dorchester."

The boyfriend's demand that Taylor meet Eliza in Boston made more sense now. Dorchester was Boston's largest neighborhood. Getting from there to Faneuil Hall wouldn't take long, and it'd be easy even with a child in tow.

Taylor went over and shook her mom awake. Neither

ringing cell phone had disturbed her. "Mom." Taylor waited for Priscilla to open her eyes. Judging by the older woman's expression, it took a moment for the previous day's events to come back. "The authorities found Eliza and Reese."

Priscilla made the sign of the cross. "Thank God. Where is she? Can we go get her?"

Taylor fixed her ponytail and yanked her sneakers back on. "The police don't have her yet."

"But you said they found them," Priscilla said.

"They did. Eliza and her boyfriend brought Reese to Dorchester. But the authorities can't burst in. They're putting a plan together." She walked away as she spoke.

"Why not? If they know where your sister and Reese are, can't they knock on the door? Demand she open it, and take Reese out?"

He knew what Taylor didn't want to share. The authorities didn't know what might be waiting for them inside. People who kidnapped a child only considered themselves. If cornered, Eliza and her boyfriend might use weapons to escape. The police, FBI agents, and HRT members didn't want any bullets finding their way into Reese or themselves.

With Taylor out of the room, Curt answered Priscilla. "The authorities need to make sure the situation remains safe for everyone, especially Reese."

He knew the moment she comprehended what he told her. "I wasn't—I should've thought of that. My husband was a police officer. But Eliza has never been a violent person. I don't think she would be now, either."

Curt disagreed. A person as desperate as Eliza might do anything, and her boyfriend was a wild card in the situation. "Then this should all be over soon, and Reese will be upstairs tucked in bed asleep."

Taylor rushed down the hall toward the front door. She held keys in one hand and Peanut, Reese's stuffed tiger, in the other. "Mom, I'll bring Reese home. Don't worry."

She'd spent enough time sitting around and doing nothing. She had a general location—Agent Morris hadn't given her a specific address—and intended to help. Go in with the team, bring Reese out, and then hand over Peanut. That wasn't the only thing motivating her, though. She wanted to be the one to slap the handcuffs on her sister and walk her to a waiting police cruiser. The Dorchester section of the city consisted of about six square miles. With a call to a friend at the Boston Police Department and some luck, she'd have the exact location soon.

Taylor never made it outside.

"Where are you going?" Curt pulled her back and slammed the front door closed at the same time.

"To get my niece. And make sure Eliza lands inside a jail cell." She yanked her arm back, but Curt kept his fingers locked around her wrist. "Please stay with Mom. Keep her company until I come back."

"Did Agent Morris share the team's location?"

She almost lied and said yes. "No. It doesn't matter. I used to work for the Boston PD and I still have friends there. I'll get the location on the way."

He stepped into her personal space. The front of his T-shirt rubbed against hers. Both understanding and compassion swam in his eyes. "Do you really think that's the best idea? Would you want someone so emotionally involved on your team when you do an arrest?"

No. This was different. She could put aside her emotions and do the job.

"It'll be better for everyone if you stay here and wait." He plucked her keys away and shoved them in a pocket before she realized his intention. Then he released her wrist and cupped her face with both hands. "When Reese is safe, they'll call us. As soon as they do, I'll bring both you and Priscilla to Reese and back home again."

"Curt, the waiting is killing me."

Curt moved closer, and she felt his heart beat against her chest. "I know. It's killing me, too." He spoke with almost as much anguish as she felt. "But let the FBI and the police and everyone else handle this. It's almost over. Reese will be safe soon."

Since Mom's first call, she'd struggled to keep everything inside, not let her fear or anger show. She needed to be strong for both Mom and Reese. Besides, crying solved nothing. It would only upset Mom more. The poor woman didn't need that. Standing near Curt, with his misery apparent, pushed her over the edge. Without warning, all the emotions she'd held back for hours broke over her and forced their way out. Tears streamed down her face, and her shoulders shook.

It's almost over. She repeated Curt's words, but they didn't soothe the fear festering inside. "Damn. I don't want to cry." She dropped her head against Curt's shoulder and his arms went around her. "It'll upset Mom more." Her words came out broken up and muffled.

"Your mom can't hear you." Curt whispered the words against her ear. "Cry all you need to. Let it out." He made small circles on her back with his hand. "You'll feel better."

Doubt that. Crying usually gave her a headache, a stuffy nose, and red eyes. But maybe a brief breakdown would help ease the tension trying to rip her body in two. Maybe after a good cry, she'd get her emotions back under control enough to get through the next couple hours.

***

Curt put to shame professional race car drivers getting them from New Hampshire to Boston after the call finally came. She'd participated in a few high-speed chases, but even she closed her eyes a time or two during the trip. And she'd heard Mom say a prayer in the back seat.

When they walked in the Boston Police Department, Captain Parker met them. "Please follow me," he said, holding open a door to a restricted area. "Reese is in a conference room with Detective Hughes. We thought she'd be more comfortable with a woman, and Detective Hughes has children around Reese's age at home."

"The poor baby must be exhausted," Priscilla said as they followed the captain.

Taylor looked down at the irregular sound of Mom's sandals bouncing off the walls. On one foot Mom wore a purple rubber-soled flip-flop, and on the other a sandal with a wooden sole. Considering how quickly they'd left the house, it wasn't a shock Mom wore mismatched shoes.

The captain opened a second door and escorted them down yet another hallway. "When I left them, Reese was talking Detective Hughes's ear off while eating a donut."

Sounds like the Reese we know and love, Taylor thought. She hoped Reese stayed that way. An ordeal like the one she'd experienced could change anyone but especially someone Reese's age.

Their escort stopped at a closed door marked Conference Room 2.

"Where are my sister and her boyfriend?" Taylor asked before the captain touched the doorknob.

When they got the call telling them Reese was safe and with the police, she hadn't asked about Eliza or her dirtbag boyfriend. At that moment, only getting to Boston and Reese had mattered. She wanted to know, though, and she didn't want it discussed in front of Reese.

"Eliza Walker and Brad Monroe are in holding. Both face a long list of charges," Captain Parker answered.

Well, she knew kidnapping was one. "What else besides kidnapping?" It'd all come out in court, but she'd rather hear it now instead of at Eliza's arraignment. Something she planned on attending Monday.

"Illegal possession of firearms. Possession of heroin."

The captain rattled off a few more charges. Taylor's mind stayed focused on the first one. Illegal possession of firearms. She offered up a little prayer. Reese and everyone who'd gone in to get her were safe, but it could've turned out much differently. Mom's expression said she was thinking the same thing.

Taylor put an arm over Mom's shoulders, and hoped Eliza spent the rest of her life in jail. "Thank you, Captain Parker. We're ready to go in."

Reese sat at the oblong conference table, half a strawberry-frosted donut and a container of chocolate milk in front of her. As she talked to the woman sitting next to her, she swiveled her chair from side to side. When she saw Taylor enter she jumped from the chair, ran over, and hugged her.

"Auntie Taylor, look what Beverly gave me." Reese stepped back and held up a white stuffed horse with a pink mane and a pink tail. A tag still attached to the animal's ear indicated it was a brand-new toy. "I named her Strawberry because her tail is pink. See?" She stretched the tail out. "And Beverly got me donuts and milk. I already ate the one with sprinkles."

Beverly must be Detective Hughes, the woman walking over to them. "I hope you don't mind. I thought Reese could use a special treat. My daughter's favorite treat is donuts."

"Reese loves them, too. Thank you." Taylor pulled Reese in for another tight hug, tempted to never let the girl leave her side again.

Reese tolerated the hug at first but then wiggled free. "Mimi, are you feeling better?" She moved and wrapped her arms around her grandmother. "Eliza said you're sick, and that I had to stay with her until you got better."

Mom kneeled so she was at Reese's level. "Don't worry about me. I'm fine."

"Good. I didn't like it with Eliza and Brad. Their house smelled really funny, and they wouldn't let me watch what I wanted. And they yelled at each other a lot."

Taylor hoped yelling was all they'd done around Reese. "Say thank you to Detective Hughes so we can go home."

"Who?" Reese asked.

"Me, silly," the detective said.

Reese waved but didn't move away from her family. "Bye. Thank you for Strawberry. I'll take good care of her." She tilted her head back. "Is Curt coming home with us?"

"I am, short stuff. I'll even give you a ride outside." He picked Reese up and sat her on his shoulders. "Ready to go?" He looked at her and Mom.

Definitely. She had the three most important people in her life around her. Everything else took a back seat. "Let's go home.

CHAPTER EIGHTEEN

She'd listened as the judge read the charges against first Brad and later Eliza. The only emotions she experienced were anger and hate. Did that make her a terrible person? Eliza was her sister. They'd grown up in the same house. They'd learned to ride their bikes and gone to camp together. Even though they'd often disagreed and Taylor hated the choices Eliza had made, she never thought she'd hate Eliza. Looking at her sister next to her court-appointed attorney, anger and hate had consumed her. She'd envisioned herself yanking Eliza to her feet and slapping her. Demanding to know why she'd done something so terrible. But she hadn't. She'd stayed silent, seated next to Mom.

Mom experienced more than hate and anger, though. She'd heard Mom sniffle once or twice as she gripped Mr. McIntyre's hand. Much like Curt, the man had been a permanent fixture at the house since Saturday, giving her the impression something more than mere friendship existed between him and Mom. If she ever got a moment alone with Mom, she'd ask her about him.

"Do you need to stop anywhere on the way home?" Mr. McIntyre asked from the front seat. He'd driven them all to Boston for Eliza's arraignment.

Mom touched Mr. McIntyre's shoulder, adding more evidence to Taylor's belief that at some point the two had started a romantic relationship. "I'm all set, Danny." Mom glanced back at her. "What about you, Taylor?"

"Good here." It'd been hard enough leaving this morning. Only the fact that Curt and Reese were together made it possible. Spending any more time away from Reese was the last thing she wanted.

Maybe that's not completely true, she thought, watching the traffic around them. Talking to Curt about what her sister had done and what it meant for them ranked pretty high on her list of things she didn't want to do.

You have to do it. She couldn't ignore the fact that Eliza tried to extort money from him. Up until now, he hadn't mentioned it or Eliza at all. Instead, after driving them home from the police station, he'd helped her tuck Reese into bed and then crashed on their sofa. Much of yesterday, he'd played soccer with them, and afterward offered to babysit today so she and Mom both could go to court. But just because he hadn't said anything didn't mean he hadn't thought about it. Once life became more normal, he might let her know he couldn't stay with someone who had such deplorable relations.

The Sherbrooke family was an integral part of elite society. The name was synonymous with wealth and prestige. People everywhere recognized it. Curt might act like the average guy next door, but his family was a vital part of him. He'd never do anything to embarrass or tarnish his family. Hell, she hated being related to someone like Eliza, but at least no one cared who her relatives were. Reporters wouldn't dig up the information and try to use it against her. However, if the media found out a member of the Sherbrooke family was dating someone who had a sister in prison, which was where Eliza would hopefully spend much of her life, it'd go nuts.

Reese kicked the white-and-pink soccer ball as Taylor

stepped out of Mr. McIntyre's car. The ball flew through the air before hitting the hood of Curt's car with a solid thump. Correction, the hood of Curt's very expensive car. He'd driven the Aston Martin to his cousin's wedding Saturday morning. When the call came about Reese, they came straight here, so his more subdued SUV remained at his Newport condo, along with her suitcase.

After hitting the car, the soccer ball bounced to the ground and rolled away. Reese shouted a hello and went after it, but Curt jogged toward her without a word to her niece about being more careful. To a man who'd been prepared to pay Eliza a million-dollar ransom, a dent in his car was probably no big deal.

"Hey, how'd it go?"

"As I expected." She preferred not to rehash today's courtroom drama. "Everything okay here?" Reese had shared very little about what happened while with Eliza and her boyfriend. And, so far, she continued to behave as she always did. Any of that could change, which was why Wednesday she had an appointment with a child psychologist her pediatrician recommended.

"Perfect. Reese went swimming and then we went for ice cream. When we got back we came out here." He searched her face. Afraid of what he might see, she looked away for a moment. "Something's wrong." His knuckles skimmed across her cheek. The tender gesture sent a sharp pain through her chest. "Do you want to talk about it? Maybe I can help."

No, she didn't want to, but what she wanted didn't matter. They had to talk, and soon. "Give me a chance to change first." She'd worn her standard court uniform: skirt, nylons, blazer, and heels. Outside of an air-conditioned building, today was proving way too warm for any of it. "I'm dying in this outfit."

"I'll be here."

Reese dribbled the soccer ball back their way. Sweat dripped down her face, and her cheeks were a nice bright shade of pink. "Why don't you both wait inside. I think Reese needs a break anyway."

Women acting unlike themselves usually didn't bode well for a relationship. While he wouldn't classify Taylor's behavior as grossly odd, something was off, and had been since yesterday. At first, he'd chalked it up to the situation with her sister and Reese. After going through such an ordeal, anyone would be distracted and distant. This afternoon it seemed more pronounced. His instincts said more than the weekend's ordeal was bothering her. Whatever the problem, he wanted to help—assuming she let him, of course. Taylor Walker was as independent as they came. Reese was quickly following in her aunt's footsteps. Taylor's strength and independence were two of the things he loved most about her, but it didn't mean he couldn't offer his aid.

"I'm having a freeze pop. Do you want one? There are blue ones." Reese skipped past him toward the kitchen. They'd spent a lot of time outside today, but she still had an overabundance of energy. An obvious perk of being a kid.

"No, thanks. Water is all I want." He was hot as hell from running around outside. The Walkers had window units throughout the home, and ceiling fans, but he missed his central air-conditioning. Any other time he would've asked Taylor to meet him back at his house. It didn't take a rocket scientist to know Taylor didn't want Reese out of hearing distance any more than necessary.

"I'll get it for you," Reese's voice floated back to him.

Curt stepped in front of the air conditioner. Cold air blew across him, and he savored the effects. After Taylor shared whatever she needed to get off her chest, he'd invite Taylor and Reese over for a swim. He hadn't gone in the pool earlier, but Reese claimed it was the perfect temperature. Priscilla could come, too, and bring along Danny McIntyre. He'd never met him before the past weekend, but it was clear the two were romantically involved.

"Much better." Taylor walked in and joined him in front of the window. She'd ditched her business attire and put on denim shorts and a blue tank top that made her eyes look more blue than gray. Not long after they met, he'd noticed how her eyes looked either bluer or grayer depending on her clothing. "Nylons are *the* worst piece of clothing ever created. I'd find a different job if I had to wear them every day."

"Try wearing a tie every day and then get back to me." Perhaps the best part of leaving Nichols was not putting a tie on each morning.

Taylor shrugged, and turned away from the blasting cold air. "Let's call it even."

"Fair enough." Sufficiently cooled off, he sat. "So do you want to share what's wrong? Maybe I can help."

She stuffed her hands into her back pockets and then pulled them out again. Her shoulders slumped slightly. He wouldn't have even known if he hadn't been watching her. Finally, she sat at the edge of the sofa, her body turned in his direction.

"It's not something you can help me with, Curt."

His insides grew uneasy at her tone.

Taylor moistened her bottom lip before she continued. "I want to apologize. No, I need to apologize."

She'd lost him. "For what?"

"My sister. For what Eliza tried to do to you. It was despicable." She spat out the last word, her anger and hate on display. "As far as I'm concerned she's dead to me. I'll never forgive her for what she did to Reese and you."

"You don't need to apologize. We don't control what other people do. Eliza and her boyfriend deserve all the blame, not you."

"And I want to thank you." She proceeded as if he'd remained silent. "For everything. Hiring the security firm, getting the money, being with me. Having you here helped me make it through this weekend."

He didn't need her thanks either. "I take care of the people important to me." Curt moved closer. When did she plan to tell him what really bothered her? Taylor's tightly fisted hands said what she'd shared so far wasn't it. "But I think you know that."

"Yeah." She cleared her throat before she continued. "That's why I understand if you decide to end our relationship."

The pain he'd experienced in his chest returned and spread. "Is that what you want?" Nothing in her behavior had prepared him for this turn in their conversation.

"*No*. Of course not." The added emphasis she put on the word no only confused him more.

"But you think I do? Why?"

"Because of Eliza. What's your family going to think when they find out my sister is in prison for kidnapping? Are they really going to want me around? I can picture the media headlines if a reporter finds out."

Okay, her logic had hopped a ride out of here. He kept the thought to himself. Instead, he'd deal with the problem and hopefully reassure her how wrong she was. "Believe me, my family's not perfect, Taylor, but they wouldn't hold Eliza's bad decisions against you. Everyone who's met you has loved you. My mother wants to know if you'll be joining us Fourth of July weekend. She wants Reese and your mom to come, too."

"That was before, Curt. She doesn't know what happened this past weekend. She might think differently when she finds out, and I don't blame her."

Her stubbornness might help when she worked a case, but right now it was a huge pain in the ass for him. "No. She won't. Neither will anyone else in my family. Trust me." He took hold of her shoulders and held her gaze. "I love you and want to be with you. That's all my family will care about. They want me happy, and you make me happy."

Curt heard flip-flops hitting the floor. "Can we go swimming?" Reese's question came in the room, announcing her arrival before she entered.

He smiled and leaned closer. "She makes me happy, too," he whispered in Taylor's ear.

"I love you." Taylor kissed his cheek, and the pain in his chest dissolved.

Later, he'd show her how much he loved her. For now he'd spend the afternoon with the two people who'd become an essential part of his life. "I'm up for a swim. Taylor, what do you think?"

"Sounds like a great idea." She glanced at Reese. "Go get your bathing suit and tell Mimi where we're going." Reese didn't need to be told twice. She zipped out of the room and up the stairs, the sound of her flip-flops echoing loudly off the hardwood floors.

"The more energy she gets out now, the sooner she'll go to bed." Taylor pressed into him. "And the sooner we can go to bed." The seductive tone told him they wouldn't be doing much sleeping.

"Agent Walker, you're a genius."

The End

I hope you enjoyed Curt and Taylor's story.

ABOUT THE AUTHOR

I started writing at the age of 10 on my grandmother's manual typewriter and never stopped. Born and raised in Lincoln, Rhode Island, I have lived in four of the six New England states since getting married in 2001. Today, I live in New Hampshire with my husband, three daughters and our dogs. When I am not driving my daughters around to their various activities or chasing around our three dogs, I am working on a story or reading a romance novel. Currently, I have two series out, The Sherbrookes of Newport and Love on The North Shore. You can visit my website www.christinatetreault.com or follow me on Facebook to learn more about my characters and to track my progress on my current writing projects.

Made in the USA
Middletown, DE
28 September 2018